"It sounds as if useful to you.*"*

Gray's unsettling brown gaze traveled from her earrings down over the stylishly simple dress to her strappy sandals. "In what way?"

"I could be your housekeeper," Clare said with a shade of defiance. "I'm perfectly capable of cooking and cleaning."

In response, Gray reached out and took hold of her hands. Turning them over, he ran his thumbs consideringly over her palms. "It doesn't look as if you do much rough work."

His touch was quite impersonal, but Clare was disconcerted to feel her skin tingling. His hands were strong, cool and calloused, and very brown against her English skin. She snatched her hands away, furious to find herself blushing.

"Herding a few cows is easy compared to looking after a baby for twenty-four hours a day!" she snapped, to cover her confusion. "I'm used to getting my hands dirty."

OUTBACK
Brides

In the hot, dusty Australian Outback,
the last thing a woman expects to find is a husband....

Clare, the Englishwoman, Ellie, the tomboy
and Lizzy, the career girl, don't come to this harsh,
beautiful land looking for love.

Yet they all find themselves saying "I do"
to a handsome Australian man of their dreams!

This month
Baby at Bushman's Creek

In March
Wedding at Waverley Creek

In May
A Bride for Barra Creek

Welcome to an exciting new trilogy by rising star
Jessica Hart

Celebrate three unexpected weddings, Australian style!

BABY AT BUSHMAN'S CREEK
Jessica Hart

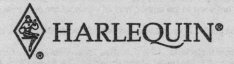

HARLEQUIN®

TORONTO • NEW YORK • LONDON
AMSTERDAM • PARIS • SYDNEY • HAMBURG
STOCKHOLM • ATHENS • TOKYO • MILAN • MADRID
PRAGUE • WARSAW • BUDAPEST • AUCKLAND

ISBN 0-373-03638-8

BABY AT BUSHMAN'S CREEK

First North American Publication 2001.

CHAPTER ONE

EYES narrowed against the glare, Clare watched the cloud of dust approaching through the shimmering haze. Could this be Gray Henderson at last?

She certainly hoped so. She had been waiting for him all morning, with nothing to do but walk Alice up and down the main street of Mathison. It had not taken long, Clare remembered with a sigh.

Apart from the hotel, there was a general store, a bank and a petrol station. A handful of low, functional houses were set in dusty yards and the whole town—if such a straggling collection of buildings could be called a town—had an air of being battened down against the heat. They had seen no one during their walk, and had retreated to the shade of the hotel verandah, where Alice had been happy enough to play with her hands and chirrup gently to herself.

Clare, though, had been heartily bored. The emergence of the dust cloud on the road that stretched emptily out to the horizon had been enough to make her get to her feet, but it was some minutes before it materialised at last into a battered utility truck. It drew up opposite the hotel with a clunk of gears, the passenger door opened and a man got out.

From her viewpoint at the top of the verandah steps, Clare could see only that he was a lean, rangy figure in moleskin trousers and a checked shirt, bending down to say something through the window to the driver. As she watched, he slapped the roof of the cab in a gesture of farewell, the truck roared off, and he turned and walked across the road towards the hotel.

The unhurried stride, the laconic way he settled his hat on his head, matched so precisely the deep, slow voice on the phone that Clare's nerves tightened with a mixture of relief that he had turned up at last and irritation. He clearly wasn't in any hurry, in spite of having kept her waiting all morning!

Not that she would be able to say anything, Clare reminded herself. She would have to be very careful. She had to get this first meeting right, not just for Alice's sake, but for her own. The realisation of just how important the next few minutes would be made Clare bend down and lift Alice into her arms, holding her small, solid body close for reassurance. Having spent the whole morning longing for Gray Henderson to arrive, she found herself suddenly hoping that it wouldn't be him at all.

But it was.

The man paused at the bottom of the steps as he caught sight of her, eyeing her narrowly for a moment before climbing them with the same infuriating lack of haste. 'Clare Marshall?' he said, and took off his hat. His gaze flickered to Alice, and his brows lifted slightly. 'I'm Gray Henderson. You wanted to see me.'

He had brown hair, brown weathered skin and a pair of unreadable brown eyes. Alice's eyes, Clare realised with a jolt. Somehow she hadn't expected that. Under their steady gaze, Clare was suddenly conscious of how strange and out of place she must look in this dusty outback town, with her pearl earrings and her yellow linen dress and her elegant Italian sandals. She had dressed with special care that morning, wanting to impress him, but if he was impressed, he was giving absolutely no sign of it.

'Yes.' She had a horrible feeling that her smile was as

brittle and alien as she looked, and her voice sounded clipped and very English compared to his slow Australian drawl. 'Thank you for coming,' she added, stilted with the effort not to ask him why it had taken him so long.

'You said it was important,' he reminded her.

'It is.'

Ever since she had learnt that she wasn't going to be able to see Jack, as she had hoped, Clare had been practising how to explain the situation to Gray Henderson, but now that he was actually there all her careful speeches had vanished, and she was left staring at him, her mind blank with panic.

If only he had been more like his brother! Pippa had told her so much about Jack's warmth and charm and reckless sense of fun that Clare almost felt that she knew him herself, and she was unprepared to deal with a man as coolly unapproachable as Gray Henderson appeared to be. Where Jack's face in photographs was mobile and smiling, Gray's was guarded, expressionless, giving her no clues as to what he was thinking.

'Shall...shall we sit down?' she suggested, playing for time while she tried to marshal her scrambled thoughts.

Gray followed her over to the bench at the back of the verandah, sat down next to her and waited calmly for her to tell him why she had asked him to meet her. It had seemed much too difficult to discuss over the phone when she had rung him last night, but now Clare wondered if it wouldn't have been easier to explain without those enigmatic brown eyes on her face.

There was something oddly intimidating about his quiet self-containment. Clare had never met anyone so unperturbed by silence. Anyone else would have explained why they were late, or even asked her what it was she wanted, but, no! He just sat there and waited.

Since he obviously wasn't going to give her an opening, Clare cleared her throat. 'This is Alice,' she said, nodding down at the baby, who was studying him with her unwinking baby's stare.

'G'day, Alice,' said Gray gravely.

He reached out to tickle her tummy with one brown finger, and Alice broke into a gummy smile that showed off her two bottom teeth. She grabbed at his finger, but lost her nerve the next moment. Overcome by shyness, she buried her face against Clare, but couldn't resist a peep back at Gray from under impossibly long lashes. When she saw that he was still watching her, she quickly hid again, burrowing closer into the safety of Clare's body.

Clare couldn't help smiling. She was prejudiced, of course, but Alice really was a beautiful baby, plump and peachy-skinned, with fine blonde hair and brown eyes. Surely even Gray wouldn't be able to resist her?

Glancing at him, she was immensely reassured to see that he was looking amused. There was a definite dent at the corner of his mouth, and a lurking smile in the brown eyes that made him look suddenly much more approachable. He prodded Alice on her tummy until she chuckled and squirmed, and Clare found herself thinking that he was much more attractive than he had seemed at first.

'How old is she?' he asked, and Clare was obscurely hurt to see that when he looked at *her* the gleam of amusement had vanished from his eyes.

'Six months,' she told him. 'Nearly seven, in fact.'

Lifting Alice off her knee, she settled her into the baby seat that doubled as a backpack when required, and forestalled any protests by offering her a floppy rabbit that had already been so sucked, pummelled, dropped and generally loved into submission that few of its original pristine features survived. She had seen Gray steal a glance at his watch. It was time to get down to business.

Unconsciously squaring her shoulders, she looked at him. Unlike Alice's, her eyes were grey, almost silvery in contrast to her smooth, dark hair. 'I suppose you're wondering what we're doing here?' she said.

'You said on the phone that you wanted to see Jack.' Gray's expression gave nothing away, but there was a shade of wariness in his voice. 'You didn't say anything about a baby.'

'No,' she admitted. 'As I told you, it's difficult to explain over the phone, and when the hotel manager gave me your number he said that you had a party line, so I thought it would be better if we could talk face to face.'

'Well, now that we *are* face to face, perhaps you could tell me what you want?' said Gray coolly.

Clare hesitated. 'It's really Jack I need to see. Do you have any idea when he'll be back?'

'A month... six weeks, maybe.'

Gray seemed unconcerned by the vagueness of his brother's plans, but Clare could only stare at him in dismay. She had been expecting him to say that Jack was in Darwin or Perth, and would be back in a matter of days. 'A *month*! But...where is he?'

'He's in Texas, buying bull semen to improve our breeding programme.'

She swallowed. 'Can you get in touch with him?'

'Not easily,' said Gray unhelpfully.

Clare's shoulders slumped as a crushing wave of exhaustion rolled over her without warning. It was more than the effect of the interminable flight from London, or the way she had lain awake the previous night worrying about how Gray Henderson would react. It was as if the strain of coping with a small baby after losing Pippa had sud-

denly caught up with her. She felt as if she hadn't slept for
months. Planning the trip to Australia had given her something to focus on, but now that she was here she was too
tired to think clearly, and the thought of trying to explain
it all to Gray was all at once too much to bear.

Bowing her head as if beneath a physical weight, Clare
clutched her hands together in her lap and forced herself to
concentrate. She *couldn't* fall apart now. 'I should have
written,' she said with an effort, her face hidden by the
slide of dark, silky hair. 'It never occurred to me that Jack
wouldn't be here.'

'If you want to leave a letter, I'll make sure Jack gets it
when he gets back,' Gray offered, almost as if against his
better judgement, but she only shook her head, defeated.

'It's too late for that. I need to talk to him now.'

'I'm afraid that's not possible, so you'll have to talk to
me instead.'

'Yes,' said Clare numbly.

Alice had dropped her rabbit, and set up a shout when
Clare didn't immediately retrieve it for her. Automatically,
Clare bent to pick it up and hand it back to her. She
couldn't think; she could just look at the baby who was
utterly dependent on her to do the right thing. Reaching
out, she stroked Alice's head, and Alice smiled trustingly
up at her as she stuffed the rabbit's ear back in her mouth.

'Look, I don't want to rush you,' said Gray after a while,
and for the first time there was an edge of impatience in
his voice, 'but I've got a thousand head of cattle in the
yards right now, and I've already given up time I can't
spare to come in and listen to you. Do you think you could
get to the point?'

Straightening, Clare turned to look at him once more.
'Alice is the point,' she said.

He frowned. 'What do you mean?'

'I mean that she is Jack's daughter,' she said steadily, 'and she needs her father.'

There was an intense silence. *'What?'* said Gray, dangerously quiet.

'Alice is Jack's daughter.'

His gaze narrowed, and he looked from Clare to Alice, who stared back at him with serious, uncannily similar eyes. One little hand held her toy to her mouth so that she could suck it, the other twiddled her ear as if to show off how versatile she was.

'Jack said nothing about this to me,' he said harshly at last.

'He doesn't know about Alice.'

'Then isn't it a little late to claim him as her father now?'

Clare pushed her hair behind her ears in an unconsciously nervous gesture. 'I think he'd want to know.'

'I think he'd have wanted to know a whole lot sooner than now if he had a child,' said Gray in a hard voice. 'If you say Alice is six months old, that means you've had a good fifteen months to decide on a father. Why wait until now to pick on Jack?'

Clare flushed. 'I haven't *picked on* him!'

'That's what it sounds like to me.' He looked her up and down almost insultingly, taking in her slightness, her tired face and the eyes that were at once surprisingly vivid and desperately sad. 'I wouldn't even have said you were Jack's type.'

'I'm not,' she admitted, smiling faintly in spite of herself. From all she had heard about Jack, she couldn't imagine that she would ever have appealed to him. She was too calm, too sensible, too different from Pippa. 'But my sister was.'

'Then Alice isn't your baby?' said Gray slowly.

'No, she's my niece.' Clare looked directly into his eyes. 'She's your niece, too.'

'And her mother?' he asked after a moment.

'My sister. Pippa.' She turned away to stare at the heat wavering above the empty road. 'She died six weeks ago,' she told Gray in a light, brittle voice, almost as if it didn't matter, almost as if her world hadn't fallen in.

There was a long silence. Beyond the shade, the sun bounced off the tin roofs and beat down on the road. A four-wheel drive, red with dust, drove past the hotel and parked a little further down, outside the general store, but that seemed to be the sum of the town's activity. To Clare, used to busy city streets, the stillness was uncanny. She could smell the dryness of the air, feel the hard bench beneath her thighs, hear her pulse booming in her ears, and she was suddenly very conscious of the man sitting quietly beside her.

'I think you'd better tell me everything,' he said.

There was something peculiarly steadying about his voice. Clare drew a long breath. She had passed the first hurdle. He would listen to her. She couldn't ask any more of him yet.

Digging in her bag, she drew out the photograph that Pippa had kept by her bed until the last. It was creased and dog-eared with handling, and Clare smoothed it out on her knee before passing it over to Gray. 'That's Pippa,' she said. 'And that's your brother with her, isn't it?'

'Yes, that's Jack,' he admitted.

He studied the picture, frowning slightly. Jack had his arm around a vibrant, lovely girl who seemed to be zinging with happiness, and they were smiling at each other as if the rest of the world had ceased to exist. 'Jack never mentioned your sister to me,' he told Clare bluntly, 'and it's not like him to be secretive.' He handed back the photograph. 'How did they meet?'

'Pippa got a job as a cook at Bushman's Creek. I'm not sure how.'

'Probably through the agency,' he said, in spite of himself. 'The station is so isolated that nobody ever stays very long, and in the dry season we always need people to help.'

If the station was anything like Mathison, Clare could imagine that no one would want to stay. 'I know she was thrilled to get the job,' she went on, unable to prevent her own mystification from creeping into her voice. 'Pippa had always dreamed about working on a real outback cattle station.'

She sighed, remembering her sister's face as she'd talked about the outback. 'Even before she left school she was talking about Australia, and as soon as she could afford the fare she got herself a working visa and came out to find a job. She started in Sydney first of all, but after a while she moved to somewhere on the Queensland coast, and then, about eighteen months ago, she wrote and said that she'd got a job on a station called Bushman's Creek.'

Clare turned to Gray as if struck for the first time. 'You can't have been there, or you would remember Pippa. She wasn't the kind of person you could forget.'

'I spent three months in South East Asia meeting buyers about eighteen months ago,' Gray admitted reluctantly. 'She could have been at Bushman's Creek then.'

'That would be about right.' She nodded. 'She was there nearly three months, and she said it was the happiest time of her life. She told me about the station, about how isolated it was and how hard everyone had to work.' Clare shook her head, remembering. 'I thought it sounded awful,' she confessed, 'but Pippa loved it.'

She paused, holding the photograph between her hands.

'And then there was Jack,' she said. 'You can see how happy they were together. Pippa said that it was love at first sight. They spent all their time together, and were talking about getting married when a row blew up one day about something quite trivial. I don't know what it was, or what was said, but I think they must have hurt each other very badly.

'Pippa was incredibly volatile. She was either ecstatic or miserable.' Clare smiled a little tiredly. 'I don't think she ever understood the meaning of moderation or balance, and she was never any good at compromising either.'

Clare glanced at Gray again. He didn't look like a man who did much compromising either, but in a quite different way from Pippa. How could she explain Pippa's intense, ebullient personality to someone like Gray?

'You have to understand what Pippa was like,' she said with an edge of desperation. 'She was passionate about everything she did. She could be the kindest, funniest, most wonderful person, and she could also be the most difficult. There was no middle way with Pippa. It was typical of her to react so dramatically when she and Jack had that argument. She thought that it meant the end of everything, and she just threw her things in a bag and came home.'

Clare sighed a little, remembering how Pippa had collapsed messily back into her own calm, ordered life. 'She didn't discover that she was pregnant until a couple of months later.'

Gray had been listening in silence, leaning forward, holding his hat loosely between his knees, but he glanced up at that. 'Why didn't she contact Jack then?'

'I tried to persuade her to write to him at least, but she wouldn't.' Clare's gaze rested on Alice, who was still happily chewing her toy and dribbling down her chin.

Reaching into her bag for a tissue, Clare wiped her face as she continued.

'Pippa was still simmering after the argument. It had been over two months, and she hadn't heard from Jack, so she assumed that he wasn't interested any more, and she was too proud to ask him for help. She thought if he knew about the baby, he'd feel pressurised into a relationship he didn't really want. I think Alice's birth made her realise just how much she still loved him, though,' Clare went on slowly. 'That was something they should have shared, and she made up her mind to come back to Australia with Alice and see if she and Jack could sort something out, but...'

Her voice wavered, and she took a deep, steadying breath. 'But a couple of months after Alice was born Pippa found a lump. She was diagnosed with cancer, and...well, she was one of the unlucky ones. There was nothing they could do for her. It was very quick.' Clare's eyes darkened with pain. 'Three months later she was dead.'

'I'm sorry,' said Gray quietly, and she sighed.

'So am I. She was such a special person. Those last terrible weeks, all she thought about was Jack and Alice. She made me promise to tell Jack how much she had loved him, and to ask him to bring their daughter up. She wanted Alice to grow up with her father in the place she had been so happy.'

'So you promised?'

Clare lifted her hands slightly and let them fall in a gesture of acceptance. 'I promised,' she said in a low voice. 'And here I am.'

Gray got to his feet and walked over to lean on the verandah rail, looking out. 'I'm not saying I don't believe you,' he said at last, 'but can you prove that Alice is Jack's daughter?'

'Why would I make it up?' she asked, bemused.

He turned to face her, folding his arms and leaning back against the rail. 'Money?' he suggested with a cynical look.

'What money? From all Pippa ever told me, you don't exactly live in the lap of luxury at Bushman's Creek!'

'We don't, but between us Jack and I own a fair chunk of land. As Jack's daughter, Alice would have a claim on that.'

Clare could hardly believe what she was hearing. 'I'm not interested in your land!' she said furiously, eyes blazing. 'What do you think I am?'

'I don't know. That's the whole point,' he said with infuriating calm. 'Until last night I'd never heard of you, or your sister, and now you expect me to believe that my brother is father to a child he knows nothing about. How do I know you're telling the truth?'

'The photograph—' she began, but he interrupted her.

'A photograph isn't proof of paternity.'

'If Jack wants to have DNA tests, he can,' said Clare, 'but I think that once he looks at Alice, he'll know that she's his daughter. You only have to look at the photo to see what he and Pippa had together, and I don't believe that Pippa would have loved anyone who could turn his back on that completely.'

'Maybe,' said Gray, clearly unconvinced, 'but that's a decision only Jack can make. You can't expect me to accept responsibility for a baby on his behalf.'

'I understand that.' Clare was feeling very tired, but she forced herself to her feet and went to lean next to him at the verandah rail. 'All I want is for you to contact Jack and ask him to come home as soon as he can. That's not too much to ask, is it?'

He looked from her to the baby, kicking her feet against the floor and squealing at the excitement of a new sensation. 'No,' he conceded, 'but it may take some time to track

him down. He didn't have a fixed itinerary, so I'll have to ring round a few contacts and hope that he turns up and gets the message sooner rather than later.'

Gray's gaze came back to rest on Clare. The straight dark hair that swung below her jaw was pushed wearily behind her ears, and there were shadows beneath the great silvery eyes. She looked bruised and exhausted, and when she looked up at him it was clear that only the stubborn strength of her will was keeping her going.

'I think it would be better if you went back to England and waited for Jack there,' he said gruffly.

Clare straightened from the rail. 'I'm not going to do that,' she told him quite simply. 'Alice and I only arrived yesterday, and even if I could face turning round and getting back on that plane for another twenty-three hours, I wouldn't. I couldn't afford to bring Alice back to Australia again when Jack finally turns up, and if he does decide to accept responsibility for her, I'd want to be able to stay with her for a while until she settles.'

'So what are you going to do?'

'Can't we come back to Bushman's Creek with you?'

There was a pause. Gray looked down into pleading eyes the colour of pale smoke and ringed with black, as if someone had taken a dark pen to outline each iris, and turned almost abruptly away.

'Bushman's Creek isn't a suitable place for you or the baby,' he said brusquely.

'Are you trying to tell me that there are no women or children in the outback?'

'I'm trying to tell you that conditions on the station are very different to what you're used to,' said Gray with an edge to his voice. 'It takes nearly forty minutes to fly there from here, and it's over two hours by road. In the Wet, the only way you can get in and out is by plane. You'd be a

very long way from shops and doctors and all the other things you probably take for granted, and, quite frankly, I haven't the time to look after you at the moment. This is one of the busiest times of the year.

'I've got fifteen thousand head of cattle out there,' he went on, nodding his head at the distant horizon. 'They've all got to be mustered in so that we can deal with them and draft out the sale cattle. The last cook-cum-housekeeper left several weeks ago, and nobody's done any cleaning since. We're taking it in turns to cook, and the kindest way to describe meals at the moment is "basic".'

He shook his head. 'I think you'd find the conditions too uncomfortable,' he told Clare bluntly. 'If you don't want to go home, you'd be better off taking Alice to one of the resorts on the coast and waiting there until Jack gets back.'

'I don't think I can afford to do that, either.' Clare flushed, humiliated at having to admit how precarious her financial situation was. 'I've got a good job at home, but Pippa had never managed to save any money, and babies are expensive little things. And then when Pippa was ill, and I had to take time off to look after her and Alice, I used up the savings I had. I bought our ticket out here on credit as it was.' She bit her lip. 'I just don't see how I could manage staying in a hotel or renting a house without knowing when Jack was going to get your message.

'Besides,' she went on bravely, 'it sounds as if I could be useful to you.'

Gray's unsettling brown gaze travelled from her earrings down over the stylishly simple dress to her strappy sandals. 'Useful?' he echoed, lifting one brow in a way that brought a flush to her cheeks. 'In what way?'

His expression didn't change, but she knew that he was amused. It was something to do with the deepening of a dent at the corner of his mouth, a creasing at the edges of

his eyes, the faintest of glimmers in the unfathomable eyes. If he thought she was funny, she thought illogically, he might at least have the decency to smile properly!

She put up her chin. 'I could be your housekeeper,' she said with a shade of defiance. 'I'm perfectly capable of cooking and cleaning.'

In response, Gray reached out and took hold of her hands. Turning them over, he ran his thumbs consideringly over her palms. 'It doesn't look as if you do very much rough work.'

His touch was quite impersonal, but Clare was disconcerted to feel her skin tingling. His hands were strong, cool and callused and very brown against the paleness of her English skin. It was as if his fingers were charged with electricity, sending tiny shocks shivering all the way up her arm, and she snatched her hands away, furious to find herself blushing.

'Herding a few cows around is easy compared to looking after a baby for twenty-four hours a day,' she snapped, to cover her confusion. 'I'm used to getting my hands dirty.'

'You're not used to the heat and the dust and the flies and the boredom,' Gray pointed out, apparently unperturbed by the way she had pulled her hands out of his. 'I'm not sure you realise how tough things can be out there.'

Not quite sure what to do with her hands now that she had freed them, Clare folded her arms in an unconsciously defensive pose. 'I'm tougher than I look,' she said.

Gray was unimpressed. 'I'm talking about physical toughness, and right now you don't look very tough to me.' He eyed Clare critically. 'You look as if you're about to collapse.'

'I've got jet-lag,' she said, wondering why she could still feel her hands burning where he had touched her. 'We only arrived in Australia yesterday morning, and I haven't been

able to rest much since then. I'll be fine after a good night's sleep.

'Look,' she went on persuasively, seeing that Gray still looked unconvinced, 'I may not be your ideal housekeeper, but you said yourself that you haven't the time to find anyone else, and I'm prepared to work hard in return for accommodation. I won't get in your way. To be honest, I'd rather have something to do to keep my mind off things.'

She hesitated. 'You've been very frank about the conditions on the station. I can't say I'm going to like it out there—I'm not like Pippa; I've never enjoyed roughing it—but I'll do whatever I have to to get to Bushman's Creek.'

'Why are you so keen to get there if you don't think you're going to like it?' he asked.

'Because I can't afford to do anything else,' said Clare, pushing her hair wearily behind her ear. 'Because I want to see the place that meant so much to Pippa. If conditions are as unsuitable as you say, it may be that I'll have to take Alice home with me, but I need to see for myself. If, on the other hand, I think it's somewhere she could grow up safely and happily, I could make sure that she's settled by the time Jack gets back. And, to be perfectly frank,' she finished, 'because I just want to stop for a while. I want to stop travelling, stop thinking, just…stop.'

'If I let you come, I don't want you to take anything for granted,' Gray warned, but she could see that he was relenting. 'Jack will have to make a decision about Alice when he gets home. Nobody else can do it for him.'

'I know.' Clare tried a smile. 'Please…?'

'Oh, all right,' he said almost irritably. 'You can come—but on one condition.'

Clare would have agreed to anything just then. 'What is it?'

'Alice's relationship to Jack has to remain secret until he

chooses to tell people about it. I don't want him coming home to find that everyone knows that he's supposedly a father except him. As far as anyone else you meet there is concerned, you're just at Bushman's Creek as a house-keeper. You rang me up last night to ask if there might be a job, and I've come in to pick you up.'

Clare thought about it. It seemed fair enough, under the circumstances. 'All right,' she agreed. It sounded a little grudging. She couldn't blame Gray for being cautious and wanting to protect his brother's interests, but at least he hadn't rejected Alice out of hand.

'Thank you,' she said gratefully, and she smiled at him.

Something flickered in the brown eyes, and he looked away as he put his hat on his head. 'If you're coming, you'd better come now,' he said in a brusque voice. 'I need to get back to the yards.'

Clare was too relieved at his agreement to object to his lack of enthusiasm. 'I just have to pack a few things,' she said hastily. 'I won't be more than a few minutes.'

Scooping Alice out of her chair, she sniffed at her cautiously. 'At least she doesn't need her nappy changing,' she said in some relief. She glanced hesitantly at Gray. 'It would be quicker if I could leave her with you,' she suggested.

After the tiniest of pauses, Gray nodded, and Clare handed Alice to him. Her hands brushed against his and she had to resist the temptation to pull them away. 'I hope she'll be OK,' she said, a little worried now as she stood back. 'She's getting to the stage where she doesn't really like being handed over to strangers.'

She lingered, uncertain whether to leave them together or not, watching as Gray held Alice at arm's length and man and baby regarded each other dubiously. Gray's eyes were intent, and Clare wondered if he were searching

Alice's small, round face for signs of a resemblance to his brother.

She was about to suggest that she took Alice with her after all when, as if at some unspoken signal, the two of them broke into simultaneous smiles. Clare was used to the way Alice's beaming smile twisted her heartstrings, but she was unprepared for the effect of Gray's. It transformed him from a brown, expressionless stranger into someone younger and warmer, someone disturbingly, unexpectedly attractive, and Clare felt oddly jolted.

There was a strange expression on Gray's face as he drew Alice into his chest and held her against him, his strong hands absurdly big on the little body. His gaze slid past the baby to Clare, who was watching them as if transfixed.

'Alice will be fine with me,' he said.

CHAPTER TWO

THE hotel was the only two-storey building in town, but its refinements went no further than a serviceable flight of stairs. There was certainly no truck with any namby-pamby nonsense like lifts or porters. Clare dragged her heavy case along the corridor and paused for breath at the top of the stairs, looking down at the scene in the entrance hall below.

Alice was looking quite at home in Gray Henderson's arms, and he was managing to carry on a conversation with the hotel manager while she explored his face with fascination, testing the texture of his skin and hair, patting his cheek and pulling at his lips.

Clare was conscious of a faint twinge of envy as she watched. It must be nice to be Alice, to be able to relax against a shoulder as firm as Gray's and to feel his hands holding her safe and secure. What would it be like to run her fingers over his face, as Alice was doing, to lean against that lean, hard body?

A slow shiver snaked its way down Clare's spine at the thought, and she swallowed, disconcerted by her own reaction. How odd, she found herself thinking, that the first man she should feel even a twinge of awareness for since Mark should be someone so completely different. Mark had been dark and intense and passionate. Gray didn't look as if he even knew what passion meant!

Except...Clare's gaze rested for a moment on his mouth. She was going to spend the next few weeks alone with this man, she realised, as if for the first time, and the shivery feeling intensified into a tight knot at the base of her spine.

23

Hastily, she bent to pick up the case. She was being ridiculous. There was no question of being physically attracted to Gray Henderson! Any amateur psychologist would tell her that his appeal was obvious. She was tired and vulnerable with the strain of coping alone for so long, and there was something very reassuring about his air of quiet strength. He might not have the looks to set her pulse racing, as Mark had, but right now the sense that he could deal calmly and competently with any situation that might arise was more appealing than any handsome face!

The hotel manager gave them a lift out to the airport in his truck. Clare was taken aback to see her things tossed unceremoniously into the back, while she was expected to squeeze into the front seat with Alice between the two men. 'How far are we going?' she asked nervously, remembering Pippa's stories about long, bumpy drives across the outback.

'Only to the airport,' said Gray, resting his arm along the back of the seat behind her head. 'It's quicker to fly than to drive, and there's usually someone around to give me a lift in to town from there.'

'Oh.' Clare was pleased to discover that she wasn't going to have to spend the next two or three hours trying not to notice the strength of his thigh pressed against hers. Not that Gray seemed to find the situation at all uncomfortable. He was talking easily across her, and Clare might as well have been a bag of shopping on the seat between them for all the notice he took of her.

It was a relief when they reached the airport and she could move away from him, although she was not impressed by the single runway set for some reason in the middle of nowhere. Clare could turn around completely and see nothing but flat brown scrub stretching off to the horizon in every direction. It was like a toy airport, she

thought disparagingly, with a windsock hanging limply in the midday heat and the 'terminal' no more than a hut offering shelter from the sun.

Gray seemed to know everybody. Even as they drove along the road, she had noticed the two men lifting fingers in greeting to the passing cars, and now, having exchanged words with the few passengers waiting for an incoming flight, he led the way across the tarmac to where a tiny plane with a propeller on its nose was parked.

'We're not going in *that*?' said Clare involuntarily.

'We certainly are.' Gray patted the plane affectionately. 'This old girl's more reliable than any car over this kind of country, and she's done this flight so often she could practically take herself home.'

Clare wasn't sure that the great age and experience of the plane was that reassuring, and in spite of her belief in Gray's competence she couldn't help closing her eyes as they sped along the airstrip, propeller blurring, and lifted lightly off the ground. She felt the plane bank and continue climbing until after a couple of minutes they levelled off.

'You can open your eyes now,' said Gray in a dry voice.

Very cautiously, Clare unscrewed her eyes. 'I've never been in such a small plane before,' she confessed. She touched the door as if afraid it would fall off. 'There doesn't seem to be much keeping us up here.'

'You're safe as houses,' he said. 'Relax and enjoy the view.'

What view? Clare wanted to ask. Spread out below them, the land stretched out to the distant horizon, as flat and featureless as a piece of sandpaper, and almost exactly the same rusty-brown colour. The sky was a huge blue glare, arching over a vast expanse of nothingness. Clare looked down at it and wondered what on earth Pippa had found to love in such barren, intimidating country.

'Is it all this…' she searched for a tactful word '…this *empty*?'

'It's not empty at all,' said Gray. 'It just looks that way from up here. You'd be surprised how different things are when you're on the ground. There's lots to see—you just have to learn to look at it in the right way.'

'Oh, yes?'

Her voice dripped polite disbelief, but Gray was unperturbed. 'You can tell you've never been outback before,' he said.

'No,' Clare sighed in agreement. This wasn't her kind of place at all. 'Municipal parks are the wildest places I usually see.'

'Not an outdoor girl, then?'

'Absolutely not,' she said, smiling faintly at the very idea. 'I've always been a city girl. Pippa was different. She couldn't wait to bump along dusty tracks and pit herself against the elements, but I never saw the appeal. Cities seem much more interesting places to me. There's always something happening, something to do, something to see.'

Gray glanced at her. 'That's what I feel about the bush.'

'It's not the same,' objected Clare. 'When you finish work, you can't go out for a meal, or a glass of wine with friends. You can't go to the theatre or a concert or an art gallery. You can't wander around the streets watching people and seeing how different they all are.'

'Is that what you do?'

She pushed her hair behind her ears with a sigh. 'It's what I used to do. I've had to put my life on hold for a bit.'

'Because of the baby?'

'Yes. She's more important at the moment.' Clare shrugged. 'I'm lucky. I've got good friends, a great flat, a job I love and a wonderful boss who's keeping my job open

for me until I can go home. They'll all still be there when I get back.'

There was a defensive, almost defiant undercurrent to her voice, as though she were trying to convince herself rather than Gray. He made no comment, asking only what she did as his eyes moved steadily between the instrument panel and the horizon and the ground below them.

'I work for an agency that represents singers and musicians,' she told him. 'I'm not musical myself—I wish I were—but I *am* good at organisation, so I deal with the administrative side of things. I love working with creative people...'

She trailed off, assailed by a rush of nostalgia. If only she were there now, in the clean, familiar office, with the gossip and the jokes and the constant, exciting buzz of activity! She was the sensible, practical one in the office, and she wondered if anyone at work would be able to imagine her now, suspended above an alien landscape in this tiny plane with a man whose stillness made her look edgy and frivolous in comparison.

'It sounds like being housekeeper on a cattle station is going to be a shock for you,' said Gray, and Clare pushed her hair wearily away from her face.

'Yes,' she agreed, too tired and homesick to make the effort to sound enthusiastic at the prospect.

'I can see why you're anxious to contact Jack,' Gray went on with something of an edge. 'The sooner you can hand over the baby, the sooner you can get back to your job.'

Clare cast him a resentful look. 'You make it sound like I can't wait to get rid of her!'

'Can you?'

Clare looked down at Alice on her lap. She was heavy with sleep, utterly relaxed as she lay in the curve of Clare's

arm, the ridiculously long baby lashes fanned over her round cheeks and her mouth working occasionally, as if she were dreaming about food. Clare could feel her breathing, and her heart ached with love for her.

'I always thought I didn't want children,' she said slowly. 'I thought a baby would be too messy, too demanding, too difficult to adapt to my job. And Alice *is* messy, and she's exhausting and all the things I was afraid she would be, but...somehow none of that matters when you've got a baby to look after. I can't imagine my life without her now.'

'If you feel like that about her, why didn't you keep her in England?' asked Gray.

'Because Pippa made me promise that I would take her to her father,' said Clare, turning in her seat to look at him. 'And because, deep down, I think it would be better for Alice to be here with him. I couldn't afford the childcare which I'd need if I wanted to look after her the way Pippa would want and continue to do my job.'

'You could give up your job,' he suggested with a cool look.

'And live on what? Pippa never had a chance to make any financial provision for Alice, and I've used up all the savings I had. I love my flat, but it's tiny. It's OK for a baby, but it would be hopeless for a toddler, and there's no garden, and I don't see how I could afford to move unless I kept my job, which takes me back to square one.'

Clare sighed. 'Believe me, I have thought about it! It's going to break my heart to say goodbye to Alice,' she said, stroking the sleeping baby's head, 'but I have to think about what's best for her. I wouldn't have brought her all the way out here unless I thought that the best thing for her was to be with her father.'

'And if Jack doesn't accept that she's his daughter?'

'Then I'll think again,' said Clare. 'But I think he will, and so do you.'

Gray's brown eyes rested briefly on her face. 'Do I?'

'I don't believe you would have agreed to let us come anywhere near Bushman's Creek if you didn't think that Jack was Alice's father,' she told him. 'I'm right, aren't I?'

Gray didn't answer immediately. His gaze dropped to Alice, and then returned to the instrument panel. 'She looks like Jack,' he admitted after a moment. 'She's got the same eyes, the same sort of look about her.

'I was away the time you said your sister was working at Bushman's Creek, so it could have happened the way you said,' he went on, as if justifying his instinct to himself. 'And Jack's been different since then. He always used to be very laid-back, but if he felt strongly about your sister and she left, that might explain why he's been moody and restless for the last year or so.'

'Didn't you ever try asking him what was wrong?' asked Clare.

'Jack's a grown man, not a kid,' said Gray repressively. 'If he had wanted to tell me what the matter was, he would have.'

Exasperated at the typically male response to any suggestion that they might discuss anything even vaguely connected to emotions, Clare rolled her eyes. 'He might just have needed you to show some interest!'

At least she had the satisfaction of provoking a reaction from Gray. His mouth tightened and the glance he gave her was distinctly unfriendly. 'I know Jack a whole lot better than you do,' he said in a curt voice. 'I would have expected him to have at least mentioned your sister when I came back, and the fact that he didn't means that I'm not prepared to make any commitment on his behalf. As far as I'm concerned, Alice is your niece, and not mine, and until

such time as Jack comes home and can decide for himself, you are just a housekeeper. Is that understood?'

Clare put up her chin. 'Perfectly,' she said.

The propeller droned remorselessly on, but inside the cabin there was a tense silence. At least, Clare felt tense. Gray looked exactly the same. He was relaxed in his seat, his hands steady on the joystick, and she eyed him resentfully.

Just a housekeeper. She wasn't sure why the comment had ruffled her. If she had to spend weeks stuck out in the middle of nowhere, she would much rather have something to do, even if it was just cooking and cleaning. Still, there was no need for Gray to make it quite so clear that he thought that was all she was good for, was there?

Why did he need a housekeeper, anyway? He obviously wasn't a romantic type, and she would have thought he would have married long ago, if only to sort out his domestic arrangements. He must be nearly forty, Clare decided, studying him from under her lashes. Surely he could have found someone to marry him? It wasn't as if he was bad-looking either, if you liked the rugged, outdoor type. His features were too irregular to be handsome, but his skin was weathered brown by the sun, and his eyes were very creased at the corners, as if he had spent long years squinting at a far horizon.

Clare's gaze travelled speculatively over the planes of his face to rest on his mouth. Nothing particularly special about his mouth either, she told herself, but then she remembered how he had looked when he had smiled, and something stirred strangely inside her, and she jerked her eyes away to stare out of the side window, as if fascinated after all by the view.

To her annoyance, the image of Gray smiling seemed to be burnt on her vision, shimmering between her and the

aching blueness of the sky no matter how hard she tried to blink it away. She might as well have been staring straight at him, Clare thought crossly.

By the time she had managed to focus on the land below, she saw that the flat expanse of scrub had given way to a range of rocky hills. The little plane climbed over them and dropped down the other side.

'Are we almost there?' she asked hopefully.

'Not yet, but we're over Bushman's Creek land now.'

To Clare's consternation, Gray dipped the nose and let the plane drop until it was barely skimming the top of the spindly gum trees. 'What are you doing?' she squeaked, clutching at Alice.

'Just having a look,' he said casually, as if it were the most normal thing in the world to take a nose-dive into the bush.

'What on earth for?' said Clare, annoyed to find that her voice was still high and squeaky with alarm.

'I want to see how many cattle are up here. There are always a few that get away from the mob when we muster.'

'Oh, we're looking for cows?' she muttered sarcastically. 'Great!'

Gray ignored her, banking the plane and swooping low over the trees. His hands were completely steady, and he seemed so in control that insensibly Clare began to relax and look around her.

At this level the featureless brown expanse resolved itself into dry, reddish earth out of which grew tussocks of grass, scrubby silver-barked gums and the occasional boab tree with its odd swollen trunk. Every now and then, a small group of cattle would blunder away at the sound of the plane, leaving clouds of dust to settle behind them, and Clare spotted several wallabies bounding effortlessly between the trees and the towering termite mounds.

'See how much more there is to see down here?' Gray asked as they dipped down over a spectacular rocky outcrop.

Clare was unimpressed. 'It's still not exactly teeming with excitement, is it?'

'I guess that depends what you find exciting,' he said. There was a faint undercurrent of amusement in his voice, and Clare looked at him suspiciously. 'What does it take to excite you?' he added with a sidelong glance.

His face was perfectly straight, but she was sure that he was laughing at her. Lifting her chin in an unconsciously haughty gesture, she met his eyes defiantly.

'More than a few lost cows and a couple of kangaroos,' she said in a tart voice. 'Is that the best Bushman's Creek has to offer?'

'That depends what you're looking for,' countered Gray, and this time she definitely saw one corner of his mouth curl upwards before he looked away.

They flew on and on, until Clare began to wonder if they were ever going to get there, but at length Gray pointed out a line of trees snaking across the landscape, their leaves notably greener than the others. 'That's the homestead creek,' he told Clare. 'Even when it's dry like it is at the moment you can still find a few waterholes. And that's the homestead down there.'

Clare peered out of the window, but she couldn't make out more than a jumble of tin roofs flashing in the harsh sunlight and shaded by a cluster of green plants and trees that looked a surprisingly lush set against the bare brown paddocks that surrounded them.

The plane dipped down over the nearby yards, where what seemed to Clare an enormous number of cattle were corralled. She could make out a couple of men who waved a greeting as the plane flew over and touched down at last,

about half a mile from the homestead, bumping to a halt on the rough airstrip.

'Welcome to Bushman's Creek,' said Gray.

Having slept peacefully through the noise and vibration of the flight, Alice woke up the moment they lifted her out of the plane. She was fractious as they got into the inevitable ute that had been left standing in the shade of a boab tree, and cried all the way back along the rough track to the homestead.

'What's wrong with her?' asked Gray, eyeing the screaming baby uneasily.

'There's nothing wrong with her,' snapped Clare, her nerves frayed by Alice's distress. 'She's hungry and she needs her nappy changed, that's all.'

She was so concerned to make Alice more comfortable that she had little time to take in much of the homestead. 'You'd better use my room,' said Gray, carrying the case into the welcome coolness of the house. 'It's the only one that's been used for a while. At least you won't have to sweep the dust away before you can find somewhere to put her down.'

His room was dim and cool and plainly furnished. There was a wide bed with a cover loosely thrown across it, a chest of drawers and a sturdy chair. The effect was one of uncluttered masculinity, quiet, comfortable and practical. Not unlike Gray himself, Clare couldn't help thinking as she laid Alice down on the bed and changed her nappy. She wished she could lie down herself, but she knew that once she did she would fall asleep. The excitement of the flight had somehow kept exhaustion at bay for a while, but now that they had finally arrived Clare felt it sweep back with a vengeance.

Bracing herself against it, Clare tucked Alice back into her clothes and picked her up. Alice's sobs had subsided

slightly, but she was still grizzly, and Clare kissed her and patted her back as she carried her in search of the kitchen. 'I know, I know, you're hungry. I'll get you some lunch.' Somehow she was going to have to get through until Alice's bedtime, she realised wearily. There was no way she could sleep while Alice needed her.

Finding herself in a large, open living area, Clare slowed and looked about her. The homestead wasn't at all as she had imagined it. It was newer than she had thought it would be, and had an improvised air, as if rooms had been added onto this central area as and when they were needed, but the atmosphere was surprisingly cool, thanks to the deep verandah that went right around the homestead and kept out any direct sunlight. Every door and window was fitted with a fine mesh screen to keep out insects but to let any breeze into the house.

Clare hadn't expected to find it such a restful house, but Gray had been right about one thing. It was badly in need of a clean. Dust lay thickly on every surface, and when she turned round she could see her own footsteps clearly marked on the floor.

'I did say it was dirty,' said Gray, appearing with the last of Clare's bags and reading her expression without any difficulty.

'I know,' said Clare. 'I just didn't realise quite how dirty you meant! Don't you possess a broom?'

'I'm hoping that you'll find it,' said Gray dryly.

'I think I'd better!' She clicked her tongue as she looked around her in dismay. 'How could you let it get into this state?'

He shrugged. 'It's a question of priorities. I only use the homestead to sleep at the moment. I'm out all day, I eat in the cookhouse with the stockmen, and if I do sit down it'll be in the office or on the verandah, never in here.'

Alice was still grizzling, and Clare cast her a harried glance. 'I'll have to worry about the cleaning later,' she told him. 'I need to feed Alice first. Where's the kitchen?'

'In here,' said Gray, leading the way. 'I'm not sure there's much to eat in here, though.'

'That's all right. I've got some jars of food for her. All I need is to be able to boil some water at the moment, and later I'll have to set up the steriliser.'

'I expect we can manage that,' he said, opening a door into a large room complete with fitted units, an enormous cooker and an array of steel fridges. 'That's where the beer's kept,' said Gray, seeing Clare's eyes follow a trail of footprints through the dust to the fridge at the end. He didn't actually smile, but the creases on either side of his mouth deepened in a way that made something shift inside Clare, and she turned away, suddenly brisk.

'Where would I find a kettle?'

'What about you?' Gray asked as she opened a jar. 'I could find you something to eat in the cookhouse,' he offered, but she shook her head.

'I'm not really hungry. A cup of tea will be fine.'

Alice was a messy eater, even by the standards of most babies, and Clare wasn't surprised when Gray left them to it after seeing what she did with the first few mouthfuls. He said that he would go and see how the men were getting on in the yards.

Clare didn't expect to see him again that afternoon, but she was just removing Alice's bib when he came back into the kitchen. 'I think there might be an old highchair somewhere,' he said, watching as Clare lifted Alice out of the backpack.

Clare's face lit up. 'Oh, that would be wonderful!' she said eagerly, and smiled at him, surprising a strange ex-

pression in the brown eyes before they were quickly veiled. 'I don't suppose there's a cot, too, is there?'

'There might be. As far as I'm aware, my mother never threw anything away, and all the stuff she used when Jack and I were small just got dumped in the unused quarters. I'll get one of the men to look them out tomorrow.'

Having taken Alice out of the backpack, Clare realised that there was nowhere to put her down. 'I think you'd better stay there until I find that brush,' she said to the baby, settling her back into the seat. Alice looked puzzled to find herself back where she had started, but she made no objection, merely sticking her fingers in her mouth and sucking them as she regarded Clare thoughtfully.

Gray was watching Clare too. She was straightening her shoulders in a gesture of unconscious weariness, and he frowned. 'You're not going to start cleaning now?' he asked sharply.

'That's what I'm here for,' she said, with a smile that somehow turned into a yawn.

'You can clean tomorrow,' said Gray in a brusque voice, looking at the smudges of exhaustion beneath her eyes. 'Right now you need some sleep,' he added bluntly.

'I can't.' Clare tucked her hair behind her ears and wished Gray hadn't even mentioned the word sleep. 'Alice slept in the plane. She'll be wide awake for hours now.'

'I'll look after her.'

Clare had the feeling that Gray had taken himself by surprise as much as her. 'You?' she said blankly.

'Why not?'

'I thought you were busy?'

'Things seem to be going all right at the yards. I'll need to go and check how they're getting on, but there's no reason why she shouldn't come with me, and in the mean-

time I've got plenty of paperwork to catch up on. She can be in the office with me.'

'But…that wasn't the arrangement,' stammered Clare. 'You don't want to be bothered with a baby.'

'I don't want to cope with her when you've collapsed with exhaustion either,' said Gray roughly. 'You're no use to me as a housekeeper if you're so tired you can hardly stand upright.'

Clare tried to push aside the tantalising prospect of being able to lie down and close her eyes. 'I don't know,' she said, worried. 'Alice can be difficult…'

'I manage four thousand square kilometres out there,' said Gray, nodding his head in the direction of the window. 'Are you telling me I can't manage a baby?'

'One baby takes just as much attention as a cattle station,' Clare pointed out. 'If not more! You can't just prop her on a fence and forget about her while you get on and do whatever you do to all those cows! You won't be able to take your eyes off her for an instant.'

'You'll have to trust me,' he said, putting an end to argument by calmly lifting Alice out of her seat once more. Then, when Clare just stood irresolutely chewing her lip, he took her arm in a firm grip with his free hand. 'Come with me.'

Clare found herself propelled back across the living area to his bedroom. 'Maybe just for an hour,' she mumbled, succumbing to temptation and the force of his will. She had held out against the exhaustion for so long that no sooner had her resistance cracked than she was overwhelmed by a great, crashing wave of tiredness, so that she stumbled and would have fallen if Gray hadn't held her up.

Beyond thinking up any more objections, or even thinking at all, she let him pull back the cover and sit her down

on the bed before he carried Alice over to the window to pull the blinds.

'Get some sleep,' he said gruffly, but when he turned to close the door behind him, Clare was still sitting there, watching him in a daze, too tired even to lie down.

Gray hesitated, then went back and set Alice down on the bed beside her. He bent and took off Clare's sandals before easing her back onto the pillow and lifting her legs up onto the bed. Covering Clare with the sheet, he picked up Alice once more and for a moment they looked down at her as she lay there like a child, looking back at them with great, blurry grey eyes.

Dimly, Clare knew that she ought to thank him, but all she could manage was a wavering smile, and by the time Gray and Alice had reached the door she was asleep.

When Clare woke, several hours later, it was to find herself lying in a strange room and a strange bed. Disorientated, she lay for a while, blinking at the unfamiliar ceiling and trying to disentangle dreams from reality in the swirl of unconnected images in her head. She was in Australia, she remembered eventually. She was at Bushman's Creek, in Gray Henderson's bed.

Gray... It was disconcerting to discover just how clearly she could picture a man she had only met for the first time that morning. Clare turned her head on the pillow as if to dislodge the memory of the creases around his eyes, the brown, competent hands, the way his uncompromising mouth had relaxed into such an unexpected smile. She had a nasty feeling Gray's smile had played an overlarge part in her dreams.

Frowning slightly as reality returned, Clare pulled herself up on the pillows. Gray hadn't wanted her to come, but he had accepted Alice in the end. He had even been kind,

offering to let her sleep, closing the blinds, even taking off her shoes.

She had a vague memory of smiling up at him and seeing the oddest expression in his eyes, but that was probably a dream, she decided. Gray wouldn't have been looking down at her with a mixture of tenderness and desire. No one would look at a housekeeper like that, and a housekeeper was all she was and all she would ever be as far as Gray was concerned.

As far as I'm concerned too, said Clare firmly to herself as she pushed back the sheet and swung her legs to the floor. She wasn't here to wonder about Gray Henderson and how he would look at a woman he really wanted to be lying in his bed. She was here for Alice, and if that meant being a housekeeper, that was what she would be.

CHAPTER THREE

CLARE was horrified to discover when she looked at her watch that she had slept for nearly five hours. Her first impulse was to rush out and find Alice, relieving Gray of the responsibility, but one look in the mirror was enough to make her change her mind. Her hair was tangled, her skin puffy and pasty and her linen dress irretrievably crushed. If Gray had coped with Alice all afternoon, he could surely cope for ten minutes longer. She *had* to have a shower!

Dressing quickly in narrow stone-coloured trousers and a white shirt, Clare felt able to face Gray Henderson once more. That sleep had done her the power of good. She felt much more like herself, she decided as she combed her wet hair behind her ears and fastened the belt of her trousers. It was time to show Gray the real Clare Marshall, crisp and capable and very different from the exhausted woman who had been too tired to take off her own shoes.

Outside, all seemed very quiet, but when Clare walked into the living area she could hear Alice's incomprehensible chatter, and she followed the sound to a room on the far side, where a door stood open. Through it, she could see Alice sitting on the floor, surrounded by an assortment of objects, as if Gray had ransacked the homestead to find anything safe that she could play with only to find his offerings discarded out of hand.

Gray himself was hunkered beside Alice, proffering a wooden spoon, and Clare was amused to note that he was looking a lot less imperturbable after five hours with his

40

small niece. He wasn't exactly pulling his hair out, but she thought that there was a distinctly frazzled edge to the way he smiled at Alice. Unnoticed in the doorway, she watched as Alice grasped the spoon and stuck one end straight in her mouth.

'There you are,' said Gray, levering himself cautiously to his feet. 'You play with that for a while, and I'll—' He broke off as Alice, having given the spoon a cursory suck, dropped it disdainfully.

'Gah!' she said in no uncertain terms.

'And I'll find you something else to play with,' he finished with a sigh.

Alice's eye fell on Clare just then, and her face split into a huge, welcoming grin. Gray had been bending to retrieve the spoon, but at her smile he glanced behind him, to see Clare standing in the doorway, looking trim and pretty. The strange, silvery-grey eyes were clear, and she was smiling lovingly back at Alice.

There was an odd little silence as he straightened and turned. 'Hullo,' he said, and there was a note in his voice that Clare couldn't identify. 'You look better.'

'I feel better,' she told him honestly, but for some reason she found she couldn't look at him directly, and it was a relief to be able to turn her attention to Alice, who was holding up her arms and babbling a greeting. The words might not make any sense, but it was clear that she wanted Clare to pick her up *now*!

Swinging her up into her arms, Clare gave her a kiss. 'Have you been good?' she asked.

'She's been...fine,' said Gray with a little reserve.

Clare glanced down at the objects scattered across the floor, and then at the desk, where an area out of the reach of baby arms had obviously been cleared. 'How much paperwork did you get done?' she asked innocently.

'Not a lot,' he admitted, and then, when Clare lifted her brows, he gave a reluctant smile. 'All right, I didn't get any done! I didn't realise one small person could restrict your activities so much!'

'Oh, Alice!' said Clare, trying not to smile. 'Have you been keeping him busy?'

'*She's* been busy,' he told her. 'I put her in the backpack and took her down to the yards, so she's met the men and seen her first cattle.'

'Wasn't she frightened?' Clare asked a little dubiously. Alice had never seen anything like a cow before, she realised, and she would have thought it would be quite alarming to be introduced to a thousand at once.

'We didn't get that close,' Gray reassured her, 'but she didn't seem to be. She never stopped talking the whole time!'

Clare tickled Alice on the nose. 'Yes, she's chatty, isn't she?'

'Can you make any sense of it?' he asked curiously.

She laughed. 'No, it doesn't mean anything. She's just making sounds—but she can usually make herself understood when she wants something! It looks as if she managed to convince you that she didn't want to sit quietly in her chair all afternoon, for instance,' she added, amused.

'Oh, yes, she got that message across all right,' said Gray with feeling. 'I tried doing some work with her sitting on my lap, but she kept throwing papers on the floor, and in any case it wasn't that easy to concentrate on figures with her chatting away, so I gave up after a while. I wasn't sure where you had packed her toys so I had to see what I could find around the homestead, but she didn't seem to be interested in anything for more than two seconds.'

'I only brought a couple of toys with me,' said Clare. 'She doesn't really play with anything at the moment.

Everyday objects are just as fascinating to her right now, but she was probably enjoying your attention more than anything else.' She hesitated, then said almost shyly, 'I'm sorry you had to give up your afternoon when you're so busy, but I really am grateful. That was the best sleep I've had in a long time. Thank you so much for looking after her.'

'That's all right,' he said gruffly. 'It was quite an education. I've done a lot, but I've never had to change a baby's nappy before.'

Clare stared at him. 'You changed her nappy?'

'With some help,' he confessed, a little shame-faced. 'I had to get Joe to show me how to do it. He's got children, but they're grown up now, and I don't think he was much of a hands-on father anyway, so he wasn't much help. In the end there were four of us standing around the bed, scratching our heads and looking from the baby to the nappy and back again. We worked it out in the end, though,' he added. 'Or we think we did! You might have to check.'

Clare couldn't help laughing at the idea of four grown men puzzling over such a simple task. 'You could have told them, couldn't you, Alice?' she smiled, swinging Alice up until she laughed too with glee.

Her laughter was so infectious that after a moment Gray gave in and laughed too. Clare's smiling glance went from Alice's merry face to his, and her heart seemed to stumble, and when her eyes met his she found her laugh faltering for some reason.

It was as if they had both realised at the same time that they were relaxed and laughing together like old friends, when they ought to be remembering that they were virtual strangers with conflicting interests and nothing in common

but one small baby. Their smiles faded simultaneously, and Clare's gaze slid away from his face.

'You should have woken me,' she said awkwardly, settling Alice on her hip.

'I looked in on you after an hour, but you were sound asleep, and I thought it would be better to leave you,' he said.

Clare didn't know whether to be glad or sorry that the impersonal note was back in his voice. It was impossible to tell what he had thought as he'd looked down at her, sprawled in sleep in the middle of his own bed.

'Well…thank you,' she said, 'and don't worry, I won't ask you to do it again!'

He shrugged slightly. 'We managed.'

'I know, but…well, the idea wasn't that you would spend your time looking after Alice while I caught up on my sleep.' She paused, choosing her words with care. 'I do appreciate what you've done today, Gray. This isn't an easy situation for you either. You've got no way of knowing whether Alice really is your niece or not, and I would have understood if you'd refused to let us come here at all, let alone give up an afternoon to entertain Alice.'

Clare took a breath and went on. 'I just want you to know that I'm grateful, and that I won't take anything for granted. You've been very kind to Alice—and to me—this afternoon, but I know it doesn't mean that you've accepted Alice as your niece. From now on, we'll try not to interfere with you.' She wished she could gauge how Gray was reacting. He was just standing there, watching her with that unreadable expression, and she could feel herself babbling like Alice, and probably making just as much sense. 'With any luck, you'll forget we're here,' she finished with a bright smile.

Gray looked at her. 'I don't think that's very likely,

somehow,' he said in his slow voice. 'I'm not sure how much use you'll be as a housekeeper if you spend your time keeping out of my way!'

'I didn't mean that.' Clare pushed her hands through her hair in frustration. At home, she was a calm, articulate administrator, with a reputation for sorting out communication problems in the office, but there was something about Gray's brown dispassionate gaze that turned her into a stammering idiot. 'I just meant...well, that I won't make any more demands on you.'

'Fine.'

Gray was straight-faced, but there was an unsettling gleam of mockery in his brown eyes and Clare's lips tightened. She was only trying to be polite and reassuring. He might at least make the effort to pretend that he took her seriously in return!

'It's getting late,' she said coldly. She was obviously going to have to work a little harder to convince him of her coolness and competence. 'I should give Alice some supper and then put her to bed. Is there a spare room we could have?'

'This way.'

He led her down the corridor and opened the door of the room opposite his own.

'But...it's clean!' said Clare stupidly as she looked around her.

'Alice and I gave it a sweep while you were sleeping,' said Gray. 'I wasn't sure what to do about Alice, but I made up the bed for you.'

She looked at the bed and had a sudden picture of Gray bending over it, his brown hand smoothing over the sheet, and colour stole up her cheeks. 'You shouldn't have bothered,' she said.

'I assumed you wouldn't want to stay in my bed,' he said in a dry voice, and her blush deepened.

'Of course not,' she said almost sharply. 'I could have made up my own bed, though.'

Gray ignored that. 'Like I said, I wasn't sure what to do about Alice. She's too small to sleep in a bed, isn't she?'

'I put her in a drawer last night.' Clare was glad of the change of subject. 'One from that chest of drawers will do fine until we can find her a cot.'

In fact, by the time Alice had been fed and bathed, she was ready to sleep anywhere, and she let Clare tuck her up in the drawer without protest. Clare pottered around the room until she was sure Alice was asleep, and then went in search of Gray.

She found him on the verandah with a shy, lanky youth introduced as Ben. Ben, it appeared, had offered to listen out for Alice while Gray took Clare over to the cookhouse for a meal.

'If you're going to do the cooking, we'll all eat in the homestead tomorrow,' said Gray as they walked over to the long, low building set a little way from the house.

Darkness had fallen with disconcerting speed while Clare had been putting Alice to bed, and she felt rather disorientated to find herself suddenly walking through the night. It was very dark, and the air was shrill with the whirring, clicking sound of invisible insects. They sounded alien to Clare, used to a background noise of traffic and sirens and voices in the street, of music played too loud in the house next door and the ticking sound of waiting taxis and the subdued roar of the planes coming in to land at Heathrow.

She imagined the eerie, empty outback stretching out all around them, and she shivered slightly, glad of Gray's tall, solid, immensely reassuring presence beside her. Clare was furious to find herself thinking that it would be even more

reassuring if she could slip her hand into his and feel his long fingers close securely around it, and, terrified that one might steal over of its own accord, she hugged her arms together.

'How many will I be cooking for?' she asked, hoping that her voice didn't sound as high and tight to Gray as it did to her.

'At the moment we've got two ringers—they're the more experienced stockmen—and four jackaroos,' he told her. 'Then, tonight, there are two truck drivers. They're taking the sale cattle out first thing tomorrow morning so they can get to the sealed road before it gets too hot. We get government inspectors occasionally, roo shooters, contractors who come in to do specific jobs...you think a place like this is isolated, but you'd be surprised how many people pass through.'

Clare had been calculating on her fingers. 'You mean I'll be catering for at least eight every night?' she said, taken aback.

'It's not a problem, is it?'

'Well, no...' she said cautiously, remembering that she had assured him that she could be useful. 'It's just I've never cooked for those kind of numbers before. I'm sure I'll manage, though,' she added quickly.

She would have to, she decided a few minutes later as she found herself ploughing through the worst meal of her life. Presented with a plate piled high with overcooked beef, stodgy potatoes and congealed gravy, Clare's confidence in her own culinary abilities soared. She couldn't do worse than this anyway, she thought, stoically chewing on a leathery piece of beef.

Clare went to bed that night feeling better than she had for a very long time, although when she wondered why she couldn't quite put her finger on the reason. The state of the

homestead appalled her, and the cookhouse had hardly been an improvement. The men around the table had been either taciturn or very shy, and their talk had been incomprehensible to her. References to scrubber bulls and poddy calves and billabongs and turkey's nests had bewildered her, and after a while she'd stopped trying to follow the conversation and let it flow over her head like a foreign language.

It hadn't exactly been her ideal dinner party, but as she'd sat there Clare had realised for the first time how lonely she had been since Pippa had died. She had been so taken up with Alice and her own grief that she had hardly seen anyone for months. At least now she had people to talk to, if she could ever work out what they were talking *about*.

And then there was Gray.

Clare had studied him, unobserved, as he'd talked with the other men on the other side of the table. Somehow it had been too difficult to look at him when he was looking at her, and she'd felt as if she was seeing him for the first time. The harsh light of a bare bulb had thrown his features into relief, and she'd let her eyes travel over the austere profile as he'd turned to talk to one of the truck drivers, drifting down from his temple to the lean planes of his cheek and the forceful set of his jaw.

It was a face at once intriguing and difficult to describe, she'd thought. There was nothing remarkable about any of his features, and the unreadability of his expression ought by rights to have made him appear dull and restrained, but somehow it didn't. Clare had been conscious instead of something quietly compelling about his stillness and his silence. He made no effort to draw attention to himself, but something about him drew the eye and made it impossible not to be aware of him.

Clare's gaze had settled at last on Gray's mouth, and she'd wondered how it was possible that its cool, quiet line

should be so familiar to her already. So familiar and yet so disquieting. It was hard to believe that she had only met him that morning. Last night she had gone to bed knowing only his name, and now...

Now she couldn't imagine not recognising him instantly, not knowing how strong his hands were, how unexpected his smile. She knew now how he walked, how he laughed, how he turned his head, and when he had looked round and caught her staring at him, it had taken a little while before Clare had realised that the cool, impenetrable brown eyes looking back at her belonged not to a man she had always known, but to someone who was to all intents and purposes a stranger.

Hot colour had surged up her throat as it had struck her how idiotic she must look, gazing across the table at him, and she'd jerked her eyes away and concentrated fiercely on her food after that.

It had been a humiliating moment, but it didn't stop Clare feeling a sense that was not *quite* happiness as she lay in the narrow bed Gray had made for her that night. It was more like relief, she decided at last, as if she had been able to put down a heavy burden and rest for a while. She had got Alice to Bushman's Creek, and she couldn't do any more until Gray managed to get in touch with Jack. When that happened, she would have to start worrying and planning for the future, but until then she would just think about one day at a time. Bushman's Creek was never going to be a place she was wonderfully happy, thought Clare as she drifted into sleep, but she could be content here, for a time.

'Content', however, was not the word to describe how Clare felt as she was dragged out of a deep sleep by Alice's cries in the early hours of the morning. 'I'm coming, I'm coming,' she mumbled, groping her way across the bedroom, too lost in sleep to decide whether it was dark be-

cause she hadn't put the light on or because she couldn't open her eyes.

She located Alice eventually, picked her up and made her way back to the bed, hoping that her touch would calm her. But it was obvious that it had taken Alice some time to wake her up, and by now she was overwrought, only redoubling her cries as Clare tried to comfort her.

With an enormous effort, Clare unglued her eyes and switched on the bedside light. It illuminated the room with no more than a dim glow, but she winced as if from a searchlight. 'All right, sweetheart,' she soothed the wailing Alice. 'I'll get you some milk. Perhaps that will help.'

The night was cooler than she had expected, and she pulled on a cotton robe before putting Alice over her shoulder and making her way along to the kitchen. Alice was screaming so loudly and the room was so unfamiliar that she had to stop for a minute and try and remember what she was doing.

'Milk,' she reminded herself aloud.

She had made up some bottles earlier, and she was trying to soothe Alice with one hand while awkwardly opening the fridge with the other when Gray appeared in the doorway, yawning and rubbing his face.

He saw Clare struggling and came over, holding out his hands. 'Shall I take her?'

Clare opened her mouth to say that she could manage, and then thought better of it. She wasn't managing very well on her own, and he was awake, so she might as well make use of him. 'Thanks,' she said, handing Alice over to him.

She watched him surreptitiously as he walked up and down the kitchen holding the baby securely against his chest. He was wearing a blue T-shirt and faded shorts, and

even in her sleep-blurred state Clare found herself noticing how strong and straight his legs were.

Soothed by the rhythmic movement, Alice's screams had subsided somewhat by the time Clare had made the bottle ready. 'Why don't you feed her?' she suggested to Gray, forgetting that only a few hours ago she had promised not to involve him in Alice's care. 'She seems happy with you.'

Gray pulled out a chair from the kitchen table and sat down. Clare watched him as he shifted Alice awkwardly into the crook of his arm and took the bottle that she offered with an uncertain glance. It was oddly comforting to see a man so competent looking at a loss for once, and she gave him an encouraging smile.

'Just offer her the bottle. She knows what to do, even if you don't!'

Sure enough, as he put the rubber teat to Alice's mouth, her tiny, dimpled hands came up to clutch at the bottle and her eyes closed as she sucked greedily.

A blissful silence fell. 'Well, that seems to be what she wanted,' said Gray, and Clare was moved to see an unmistakable expression of tenderness on his face as he looked down at the baby lying trustfully in his arms. 'Does she wake up like this every night?'

'No, but it's upsetting for her to be out of her normal routine.' Clare dropped into the chair next to Gray's and regarded Alice with a mixture of concern and love tinged with bewilderment at how quickly the baby had switched from sound and fury to this picture of quiet innocence. Alice's lashes were still spiky with tears, but the hectic flush was already fading and she looked remarkably content as she lay back in Gray's arm. 'I should have expected her to wake tonight.'

Leaning back in her chair, she ran her fingers tiredly

through her hair. 'I'm sorry we woke you,' she yawned. 'You'll have to put a pillow over your ears next time.'

'I'm a light sleeper,' was all Gray said.

Alice was getting too greedy, the milk beginning to bubble at her mouth, and without being prompted Gray took the bottle away and wiped the froth with his thumb.

'You're a natural,' said Clare, watching the gentle movement of his hands. 'I wonder if it's because you're so calm?' she went on, lulled by the intimacy of the night into betraying thoughts that would have been concealed in the bright light of day. 'Babies can tell if you're tense and worried about something. You must have a nice, slow, steady heartbeat.'

Gray's eyes rested on her for a moment. Her silky hair was tousled, her eyes soft and drowsy with sleep, and he could see the warm flesh of her throat, the full curve of her breasts outlined beneath the softly draping robe.

He offered Alice the teat of the bottle once more. 'Not always,' he said in a dry voice.

Too tired to feel awkward with him, Clare leant on the table, her chin propped on one hand, happy simply to listen to Alice guzzling contentedly in the quiet room. She showed Gray how to burp her, and watched him get the hang of it at once. 'Are you sure you've never done this before?' she asked, half joking.

He shook his head. 'No, but one of my earliest memories is of my mother giving Jack a bottle in this very kitchen.' He thought back. 'I must have been five or so.'

Pippa had said that Jack was thirty-three. Considering that it was the middle of the night, Clare didn't think it took her too long to work out that that meant Gray was thirty-eight. 'That's quite a big gap,' she commented. 'Are you close?'

'When you grow up in a place like this, there aren't any

other children to play with, so you don't have much choice but to be close,' said Gray. 'We used to do lots together. We always got on well,' he remembered. 'When our parents died a few years ago, it seemed natural to carry on running the station between us.'

'You don't seem at all alike.'

Clare spoke without thinking and Gray lifted an eyebrow. 'I didn't think you'd met Jack?'

'I haven't, but I heard about him from Pippa. He sounds wonderful,' she said, thinking of the stories Pippa had told. 'Warm, funny, exciting…' Belatedly, Clare realised what she was implying, and she blushed. 'That is…I don't mean that *you're* not…'

She trailed off in embarrassment as Gray glanced up from Alice, but was relieved to see that he looked amused rather than offended. His eyes were creased at the corners and there was a definite twitch at one end of his long, cool mouth.

'No, you're quite right,' he agreed gravely. 'We are quite different! Jack has always been much more easy-going than me, but more reckless, too. He was always getting into trouble when he was younger, although he was pretty good at getting out of it as well. He could charm the birds off the trees when he wanted!'

'Pippa was like that,' said Clare. 'She was like our father. They were both hopelessly romantic, and prone to wild, extravagant ideas that never quite worked out the way they planned, but they were so much fun to be with that no one ever minded.'

She smiled reminiscently. 'I was the sensible one of the family. My mother died when I was thirteen, and I suppose I automatically stepped into her shoes. Dad and Pippa used to tease me about how practical I was, but someone had to

look after them. They would never have managed on their own.'

'Is your father still alive?' asked Gray, and she shook her head.

'No, he died seven years ago.'

He frowned slightly. 'So now you're on your own?'

Clare's gaze rested on the baby in his arms. 'Now there's Alice,' she said.

There was a pause. 'It must have been very hard for you when your sister died,' he said quietly.

'Yes.' Clare sighed, and she looked out of the window at the night. 'Yes, it was. When she died, I felt as if a bit of me had died too. Pippa was always so vivid, so *alive*. I still can't quite believe that she won't come breezing back and announce that she wants to sail round the world or go and live in the rainforest and make jewellery. I always envied her her ability to live for the moment. Pippa didn't waste her time planning or saving for the future. Until she met Jack, all she ever wanted was to live dangerously.'

'And what did you want?'

'Security.' She flushed slightly as she looked back at Gray. 'It sounds so boring, doesn't it? Dad was always changing jobs, and when we were children we spent our whole time moving from school to school. It gave Pippa incurably itchy feet, but I used to long to stay somewhere long enough to put down some roots and belong.

'I bought a home of my own as soon as I could afford a mortgage,' she went on. 'Pippa couldn't understand how I could be happy staying with the same agency I've worked for since I was twenty-one, but I love going back to my flat every evening. I like getting the same bus in the morning, working in the same place, seeing the same people.'

Gray was watching her with a curious expression, and Clare put up her chin, unaware of the way her wide, pas-

sionate mouth belied the calmness of her clear grey eyes. 'I suppose you think I'm boring too?' she said with a shade of defiance.

'That's not what I was thinking, no,' he said slowly.

When she thought about their conversation the next morning, Clare was aghast. She must have been half asleep, she decided, her defences down in the dark, or she would never have sat there making stupid comments about Gray, about his heartbeat, and how good he was with babies. She couldn't have sounded more like a desperate woman if she had tried!

Clare cringed at the memory. What if Gray thought she was trying to flirt with him? What if he thought she was so wrapped up in babies that she was determined to have one of her own, and had singled him out as good father material?

'I'm just going to have to impress on him that I'm a career girl,' she told Alice as she changed her nappy, 'and that if I *do* ever think about another man, he'll need to have more than a steady heartbeat to recommend him!'

Alice chortled and kicked her legs in support, and Clare tickled her tummy. 'So you think all I've got to do is convince him that I'm not really the kind of girl who goes all gooey-eyed the moment a man picks up a baby?'

'Ma!' said Alice, which Clare took to mean yes.

No more intimate discussions, she resolved. She would be friendly, polite, of course, but reserved—rather like Gray himself, in fact. The thought made Clare frown slightly. Why was she working herself into a state? She was prepared to bet that Gray wasn't wondering whether he had given *her* the wrong impression last night!

She prepared a cool greeting as she carried Alice along to the kitchen, and was perversely cross when she discov-

ered that Gray wasn't there to be impressed by her composure. It was only seven o'clock, but he was clearly long gone.

Clare read the note he had left on the kitchen table. It said only that they were loading the trucks and would be back for smoko later that morning, and she sighed. No comment about the fact that she was sound asleep when she should have been cooking breakfast for him and the other men, but Clare was sure he must have thought it. So much for impressing him with her professionalism!

It wouldn't happen again, she vowed, and to make up for her first failure she threw herself into cleaning the kitchen. She might not have been much of a cook as yet, but she would show Gray that he would have no cause to complain about her as a housekeeper!

When Gray came back over three hours later, Clare was on her knees scrubbing the kitchen floor, while Alice was happily occupied with a plastic cup and a bowl of water. 'You've been busy,' he said in greeting, lifting his brows as he looked around the kitchen.

Clare's head jerked up at the sound of his voice. Gray was lounging in the doorway, looking somehow even more definite than she had remembered, and her heart seemed to turn over at the sight of him, leaving her stupidly breathless. Just surprise, she told herself firmly.

She sat back on her heels, wiping her face with the back of her arm. 'Did you think I would still be in bed?' she asked, more sharply than she had intended.

If Gray noticed the tartness in her voice, he gave no sign of it. 'No,' he said calmly, 'but I didn't expect to find you down on your hands and knees, either.'

'I'm here to work,' she reminded him in a haughty voice.

Gray didn't say anything, but Clare was sure that she could detect a lurking amusement in his eyes, and she was

suddenly very conscious of how she must look to him with her hair sticking to her head, smudges of dust on her red face and her shirt damp and dirty. No doubt he was comparing her grubby appearance with the way she had looked yesterday, when she had assured him that she was used to hard work!

'What are you doing back here, anyway?' she asked crossly.

'We've just finished in the yards,' he answered. 'The boys are having a smoke outside, and I came to make some tea. If it's all right for me to walk on your clean floor, of course?'

What was it about him that made her so convinced that he was laughing at her when his face was perfectly straight? Clare clambered to her feet, feeling ruffled without knowing why. 'I'll do it,' she said tightly. 'It's my job, after all.'

Gray watched her fill the kettle and shove in the plug with unnecessary force. 'You seem to be very keen on your job today,' he commented.

Laying his hat on the side, he propped himself against a unit by the door, arms folded and long legs crossed at the ankles in front of him. His boots were dusty, the sleeves of his checked shirt rolled casually back to reveal strong, brown wrists. He looked completely relaxed, but Clare was aware as never before of the leashed power of his body.

Averting her eyes, she rummaged in the cupboard for some tea. 'I don't think "keen" is the right word,' she said, willing the kettle to boil quickly.

'What is the right word?'

She shrugged. 'Resigned?' she suggested. 'I can't say scrubbing floors is my ideal job! I'm used to a little more mental stimulation and rather nicer surroundings!'

'You wanted to be housekeeper,' Gray pointed out.

'Only because it was the only way to get here,' Clare

retorted without thinking. She saw Gray's brows draw together, and wished suddenly that she had been more tactful. 'You don't need to worry, though,' she added quickly. 'I'm planning to keep my side of the bargain. I wouldn't have spent the whole morning on my knees if I wasn't prepared to do what I said I was going to do, would I?'

She looked out of the window by the kettle. Beyond the shade of the verandah, the bush stretched interminably off into the distance. 'It's not as if there's anything else to do,' she added with a sigh.

Gray levered himself away abruptly from the unit. 'Well, with any luck you won't have to put up with it all much longer,' he said curtly. 'I rang a number of contacts in the States before I went out this morning. It was a good time to get hold of people.'

Jerked out of her contemplation of the boredom stretching ahead of her, Clare spun round from the window. 'Did you speak to Jack?' she asked eagerly.

'No, but I left a message for him with everyone I spoke to, so they'll pass it on as soon as he gets in touch. That should be any day now.'

Clare looked down at Alice, who was busy splashing water all over the floor, oblivious to her own future. 'Let's hope so,' she said.

'In the meantime,' said Gray, 'you are, as you pointed out, here as housekeeper.' There was an implacable note in his voice that Clare hadn't heard before. 'That means you'll need to provide a meal tonight. Cold meat and bread will be enough for lunch, but the men like something sweet for smoko in the mornings and afternoons. Perhaps when you've finished the floor you could make some biscuits or a cake or something.'

It was an order rather than a request, and Clare looked at him in disbelief.

'But there's still the rest of the house to clean, not to mention Alice! When am I going to have the time to do some baking?'

'You were the one who said that you didn't have anything else to do,' Gray pointed out unfairly. He picked up his hat. 'I'll be out on the verandah when the tea's ready.'

CHAPTER FOUR

'I've had enough!' Clare declared, fitting a floppy hat on Alice's head. 'We've got to get out of this kitchen!'

Stung by the way Gray had implied that she might not be able to cope after all, she was determined to prove that she would be the best housekeeper they had ever had at Bushman's Creek. An inspection of the storeroom had revealed the wherewithal to make not only a chocolate cake for afternoon smoko but flapjacks as well. In between, Clare had finished cleaning the kitchen and swept the living area. She had provided lunch for one small baby and seven big men, and cleared up after them all, and now it was *her* turn for a break.

'Come on, Alice,' she said as she settled her into the backpack. 'You and I are going for a walk.'

Outside, the air was hot and dry, and the light so bright after the shady homestead that Clare had to screw up her eyes against the glare. She hesitated at the bottom of the verandah steps. To one side lay the creek, which as far as Clare could see consisted of a few trees leaning over a dry riverbed. Shady, but dull, she decided. To the other side was the cookhouse, flanked by two long, low buildings which were apparently the stockmen's quarters. Perhaps there would be more to see that way.

There wasn't. Clare and Alice inspected a wind tower, its blades unmoving in the hot, still air, two big water tanks, a radio mast and sundry other dilapidated-looking sheds, but that seemed to be about it.

Oh, and a chicken run, Clare discovered as she walked

on. They watched the hens scratching around in the dust for a while, but even this welcome sign of activity palled after a while. It was all so brown, so bare, so *boring*, thought Clare disparagingly.

And so hot.

And so full of flies.

Waving them away from Alice's face with a sigh, Clare carried on down the track which led to the cattle yards. There seemed to be a lot of bellowing and shouting going on, so *something* must be happening. It would make a change from chickens, anyway.

Rounding a bend in the track, she found herself confronting a scene of apparent confusion. There was a lot of dust swirling in the air, and it was hard to make out what was going on at first, but, after Clare's first appalled thought that she had arrived in time to witness a stampede, she realised that the men were deliberately moving the cattle out across a bare brown paddock behind.

Once she was sure that they were going in the opposite direction, Clare walked closer and watched the men chivvying the last of the cattle out of the yards. She spotted Joe's wiry figure, and a couple of the jackaroos on horses, making sure that the herd stayed together, but there was no sign of Gray.

Obscurely disappointed, Clare turned and set off back to the homestead. The creek might have been more interesting after all.

She had only gone a little way when she heard the sound of hooves behind her, and, looking over her shoulder, saw Gray cantering up on a huge chestnut horse with a white blaze down its nose. To Clare's alarm, it was snorting and tossing its head, but Gray seemed to be able to handle it without effort, sitting easily in the saddle, reins held in one strong hand.

Still, Clare stepped nervously out of the way as he reined the horse in. She looked up at him from the edge of the track, and for a strange moment felt almost giddy, as if the earth were spinning slowly beneath her feet. It was something to do with the powerful, sidling horse, something to do with the clarity of light and the way Gray was outlined against the glaring sky. The shadow of his hat fell across his face, but she could see the long, quiet mouth, the faint stubble on his jaw, the tendons in his hand as he controlled the horse, all etched with a startling intensity that stuck the breath in her throat.

'Did you want me?' he asked, and Clare stiffened.

'Want you?' she echoed defensively. 'Certainly not! Why should I want you?'

'I don't know. That's what I came to find out.' Gray swung himself out of the saddle and pulled the reins over the horse's head. 'Ben said he had seen you down by the yards and he thought you might be looking for me.'

'Well, I wasn't!' Clare was ruffled, more unnerved than she wanted to admit by the man standing in front of her, by his easy competence and his smile that wasn't quite a real smile, by the way he made her feel. 'I wasn't looking for anyone, and if I *had* been, I don't see why you should assume it would have been you!'

She knew she sounded unreasonable, but Gray was a hard man to provoke. The horse nickered, and he put up a hand to soothe it. 'Something might have been wrong,' he said calmly.

'Nothing's wrong,' snapped Clare. 'I'm entitled to a break, aren't I? I just thought I'd come out and have a look around. Have you got any objections?'

'Only to you wandering around without a hat,' he said. 'You put one on Alice. Why didn't you wear one yourself?'

'I haven't got a hat,' she said a little sulkily. 'I didn't

really think about my own clothes when I was packing. I suppose I thought I could buy one when I got here if I needed it. That was before I realised it was five hundred miles to the nearest hat shop, of course,' she added with a touch of sarcasm.

'There are plenty of hats in the homestead. I'll find you one this evening.' Gray took off his hat and had placed it on Clare's head before she had a chance to protest. 'In the meantime, you'd better wear this.'

It felt strange and oddly intimate to be wearing his hat. It was too big for her, and Clare put up an uncertain hand to the brim. 'It's really not necessary,' she said, disconcerted. 'I'm going back now.'

'Wear it anyway,' he said. 'You're not used to the sun.'

'We do occasionally see the sun in England, you know!'

'Not like this,' said Gray.

That was undeniable, thought Clare with an inward sigh. The hottest English summer had nothing to compare with this relentless heat and light.

The horse snorted and shook the flies from its mane, nudging Gray as if impatient to move on, but he ignored it. 'So, what do you think?' he asked Clare.

She eyed him suspiciously. 'About what?'

'About Bushman's Creek.'

'To be quite honest, I can't imagine why Pippa loved it so much here,' she said frankly.

Gray looked around him as if trying to see things through her eyes. 'I guess it's a bit different from home for you,' he agreed.

Clare thought about the street where she lived, where the terraced houses faced each other, neat and unpretentious, but given character by their painted doors and window boxes and tiny, carefully tended front gardens. In spring, the cherry trees lining the street were laden with blossom,

and on summer evenings you could sit outside the friendly pub at the end of the road and enjoy a drink in the long twilight. It was hard to imagine anywhere more different from Bushman's Creek.

Remembering her home, Clare had a sudden, intense longing to be there, where everything was safe and familiar, instead of in this wild, sunburnt country. At home, the light was soft and the grass lush and green. There were no clouds of flies, no dusty tracks stretching out to the horizon, no unsettling men with slow smiles and strong hands and eyes that were creased at the corners from years of squinting at the sun.

'It is a bit,' she said with a sigh.

'You get used to it after a while.'

Absently, Gray stroked the horse's nose. Clare found herself watching the long brown fingers, as if fascinated, and when he glanced up she had to wrench her eyes away, flushing.

'I can't imagine ever getting used to it,' she said. 'It's all so….so *intimidating*. There's too much of everything. Too much heat, too much sky, too many flies—but not enough to see and not enough to do. It's just big, brown nothingness!'

'You can't dismiss Bushman's Creek after a five-minute stroll.' There was a tight look to Gray's mouth now. 'You haven't seen anything yet. Wait till you've seen the water-holes and the ranges and the gorge up the top end. Wait till you've seen the rains come and the creeks in full flood and the grass growing up to your waist. You won't think the station's brown or empty then!'

Clare looked unconvinced. 'I don't expect I'll get the chance,' she said airily, spotting a chance to reassure him once and for all that last night she had been behaving com-

pletely out of character. 'No doubt Jack will be back before then.'

'And you can't wait to shake the dust of Bushman's Creek off your shoes, is that right?'

'Well, it's not really my kind of place,' she told him. 'And, after cleaning your kitchen, I never want to see any kind of dust anywhere ever again!'

Gray looked at her as if debating with himself whether it was worth arguing with her, but he obviously decided it wasn't, and Clare couldn't help feeling rather cheated as he threw the reins back over the horse's head and swung effortlessly back into the saddle.

'If boredom's your only problem, I might as well get back to work,' he said in a dry voice. 'We'll be back for smoko in about an hour and a half.' He turned the horse around and glanced down at Clare, looking up at him with her silver eyes full of sunshine. 'Don't let me catch you out without a hat again,' he said, and, touching his heels to the horse's side, he cantered away.

Clare watched him until he had disappeared round the bend in the track and the dust had settled behind him. Then she turned with a tiny sigh, straightened his hat on her head, and made her way slowly back to the homestead.

'You look tired.'

The rough note in Gray's voice made Clare look up in surprise from where she was wiping down the kitchen table after the evening meal. 'I'm fine,' she said automatically, although her feet ached and her whole body was buzzing with tiredness. She might have told Gray that she was used to working hard, but she wasn't used to working quite *that* hard all day.

'You've done enough for today,' he said. 'You've earned

some time off. Go and sit on the verandah, and I'll bring you a cup of coffee.'

The thought was too tempting to resist. 'All right,' said Clare, rinsing out the cloth and avoiding Gray's eyes. 'Thank you.'

She didn't know how to react to Gray now, she thought as she dropped into one of the big verandah chairs with a sigh of relief and closed her eyes. She couldn't help wishing that she hadn't been *quite* so disparaging about Bushman's Creek now. It was all very well being honest, but she could have been more tactful. It was Gray's home, after all, and he had been more helpful than she deserved, not only feeding Alice for her, but sending Joe to look out the highchair and an old cot which he had promised to refurbish.

Looking back to that afternoon, Clare couldn't understand why she had been so thrown when Gray had appeared like that on his horse. She had been so anxious to convince him that he had the wrong impression of her after the previous night that she had ended up convincing him that instead of being desperately in search of a man she was rude and silly, and now he still had the wrong impression of her, even if it was a different one!

Clare gave a sigh that turned into a yawn. Conscious of her own rudeness, she had been secretly nervous about seeing Gray again. She wouldn't have blamed him if he had told her that she could go if she felt like that about Bushman's Creek, but in the event he had made no reference to their conversation at all when they'd come in for afternoon smoko. He had just carried on exactly as before—which meant that she had absolutely no idea what he was thinking or feeling.

At least the cake and the flapjacks had gone down well, Clare reassured herself. And, after all, what did it matter

what Gray thought of her? The main thing was what he thought about Alice, and it was obvious that he had already accepted her as part of his family and was a fair way to being besotted. After showering that evening, he had come into the kitchen to find Clare trying to feed Alice with one hand and peel potatoes for eight with the other.

'Let me feed her,' he had offered, as Alice gave him a beaming if somewhat messy smile of welcome.

Clare looked at him warily, reluctant to break her side of the bargain by seeming too eager to hand over responsibility for Alice. 'You don't have to—' she began, but Gray interrupted.

'I'd like to,' he said gruffly. 'She's my niece as well as yours, and if she's going to stay here I might as well learn to do my share.'

It was the first time he had acknowledged Alice as Jack's daughter, and Clare felt a great wave of relief wash over her. She loved Alice dearly, but it had been lonely having sole responsibility for her. Now at least there was someone else to share the worry.

'She's a very messy eater,' she warned Gray, handing over the spoon. 'You might wish you'd waited to have your shower!'

Alice had a spoon of her own, which she waved around and occasionally splattered into her bowl, but generally preferred to dabble her fingers in the purée Clare had made specially for her. Clare was used to the way she then wiped them over her hair and face, but it was obvious that Gray hadn't bargained for quite so much mess. If he had thought that feeding his niece would be a simple matter of spooning food into her mouth, it took no time at all to disillusion him!

Clare couldn't help laughing at his expression as his attempts to help Alice were imperiously rejected, and the

faint strain in the atmosphere dissolved as Gray glanced helplessly at her.

'Do you think she's eaten anything at all? I seem to be wearing most of her food!'

She left him to recover while she bathed Alice, but when she was clean and sweet-smelling once more, she took her back to say goodnight. Alice stretched out her arms as soon as she saw Gray, and as Clare handed her over to him she saw an expression in his eyes that made her throat tighten, and she looked quickly away.

Now, Clare lay back in her chair on the verandah and wondered about Gray. His quiet reserve should have made him boring, but instead there was something intimidating about his capacity for stillness and silence, something unsettling about those unfathomable brown eyes. And then, just when she thought she could dismiss him as a strong, silent type, he would surprise her with unexpected tenderness.

Alice trusted him. By rights, she should have been wary of a strange, silent man who had no experience of children, but she had taken to him at once. Something that was not quite jealousy stirred inside Clare when she remembered Alice's tiny hand clutching his finger, the way she had gurgled with pleasure and held out her arms, confident that he would love her, the way his mouth had curved as he'd kissed her smooth baby cheek.

Lucky Alice. The thought slid insidiously into Clare's mind, and her eyes flew open to see Gray watching her with a peculiar expression.

'Sorry, I didn't mean to disturb you,' he said as she jerked upright. He set a mug of coffee down on the table beside her. 'Were you asleep?'

'No.' Clare was horrified to hear how husky her voice

sounded, and she hurriedly cleared her throat. 'Just think-ing.'

'What about?'

Gray switched off the lights, leaving only the strange glow of the blue fluorescent light in the yard, which was designed to draw insects away from the house. It snapped and sizzled occasionally as flying bugs blundered into its trap.

Clare was glad of the darkness as he sat down beside her. She wondered what Gray would say if she told him she had been thinking about him, and how his lips would feel against her skin.

'Oh, just that Alice seems to like you,' she said carefully instead. She turned to look at him through the darkness. 'You're very good with babies. Haven't you ever wanted any of your own?'

Gray considered the question, sitting forward in the chair, the mug of coffee held between his hands. 'I've never really thought about it,' he said after a while. 'I guess I assumed that Lizzy and I would have kids eventually.'

There was a strange feeling in the pit of Clare's stomach. 'Lizzy?' she echoed, a little too sharply. 'Who's Lizzy?'

'A friend of mine,' said Gray. 'Her parents live on a property the other side of Mathison. We've known each other since we were kids.'

'Oh.' Clare digested this. 'So you were childhood sweet-hearts?' she prompted, hoping that he wouldn't think that she was being too nosy.

'I guess you could say that,' he agreed. 'We were en-gaged for a while a few years back.'

Gray? Engaged? Why did the thought make her feel so edgy? Clare picked up her coffee and sipped it while she tried to adjust to the idea. It wasn't as if it was that sur-prising, was it? She had wondered herself why he wasn't

married, so why should she feel different now that she knew that there *had* been someone who had been able to break through that enigmatic reserve?

'What happened?' she asked curiously.

'Nothing dramatic,' said Gray with a sidelong glance. 'We were both young, and Lizzy wanted to go and work in Perth before we got married.'

'Did she...did she meet someone else?'

'No.' Gray's voice was very dry. 'She just loved living in a city and she loved her job. When she came home, she said it wasn't the same any more. She couldn't face spending the rest of her life in the outback, and I couldn't face leaving it, so we agreed to go back to being friends. No big tragedy.'

'But...didn't you mind?' stammered Clare, thrown by his dispassionate account. He must have felt *something*, surely?

'I wasn't bitter, if that's what you mean. I couldn't feel bitter about Lizzy even if I wanted to. She's one of my best friends. She always has been and she always will be. I'm glad she had the guts to tell me how she felt before we made a terrible mistake.'

His voice was warmer than she had ever heard it. Clare curled her fingers around her mug, conscious of an odd pang. It sounded as if Gray was still in love with Lizzy.

'Perhaps she'll change her mind and come back to you,' she said.

'I don't think so,' said Gray evenly. 'Not now. She's a city girl now, and this is still the outback.' His eyes rested on Clare's profile, pale and blurry in the dim light. 'I'd have thought you would have understood Lizzy's point of view better than anyone.'

Clare was startled. 'Me?'

'You wouldn't be prepared to live out here either, would you?'

'I'm not in love with you,' she pointed out after only the tiniest hesitation.

'Imagine that you were,' he told her, 'and that I were in love with you. Would being in love make up for the heat and the flies and the isolation?'

Clare swallowed, alarmed at how easily she *could* imagine it. If she were in love with Gray, they would sit close together in the dark, and she would know exactly what it felt like to kiss him. She would be utterly familiar with his smile, with his hands, with his lean, hard body. She would feel very safe if Gray loved her, Clare found herself thinking. She would wake every morning in his big, comfortable bed and know that he would always there.

And so would the flies, and the eerie stillness, and the empty, unchanging horizon.

'Of course not,' she said. 'But I'm a stranger. I'm not used to the outback. Lizzy grew up here.'

'All the more reason for her to know exactly what marriage to me would mean,' said Gray.

'You're very quick to defend her,' said Clare, aware too late of the accusing note in her voice. 'Lizzy must mean a lot to you.'

'She does.'

There was a curt edge to his reply, and her interest quickened. So he *was* still in love with Lizzy! Clare couldn't help wondering about the girl he had fallen in love with, the girl he had never been able to replace. What did it take to hold a man like Gray for all those years?

'What's she like?' she asked curiously.

'Lizzy? She's the kind of person who lights up a room when she walks into it. She's very warm, very generous, intensely sociable.' Gray smiled, and Clare had the feeling

that he had forgotten that she was even there for a moment. 'Lizzy was born to party,' he went on. 'It doesn't matter where she is or who she's with, she's always having a good time.' He glanced at Clare. 'You'd like her. Everybody does.'

Clare wasn't so sure that she *would* like Lizzy, somehow. She shifted uncomfortably in her seat, feeling disgruntled for some reason. She had never been much of a party girl. Was it just coincidence, or had Gray made a point of explaining how different Lizzy was from her?

'If she loves parties, I can see why she wouldn't want to live in the outback,' she said, hoping that she sounded cool rather than cross. 'It's a pity we can't all make sure we fall in love with suitable people, isn't it? You need someone homely and down to earth, who hates crowds and enjoys housework.'

'Do I?' said Gray, expressionless. 'And what about you, Clare? What do you need?'

Clare looked out at the darkness. It was very still, and the night air was loud with whirring and clicking, interspersed by the sudden snap of the blue light as it claimed another victim. She had been trying so hard not to think about Mark at all. Part of her wanted to keep her feelings secret, but another part longed to talk about him, just to say his name aloud. Gray had told her about his hopeless love, so perhaps it was only fair to tell him about hers.

'I need someone I can't have,' she said bleakly.

'Why not?'

'Oh, usual story,' she said, trying to sound light but unable to keep the bitterness from lacing her voice. 'I made the mistake of falling in love with a married man.'

'I see.'

Gray's voice was carefully neutral, but Clare turned towards him almost defensively.

'I didn't know!' she cried. 'I wasn't expecting to fall in love. I was thirty. I didn't think it would ever happen to me.' Linking her hands in her lap, she made an effort to steady her voice. 'I had my job, I had my flat, I had my friends,' she tried to explain. 'I was happy. And then one day Mark walked into the office, and it was as if every love song had been written specially for me.'

She smiled a little wearily, remembering that wonderful day. 'I know it's a cliché, but that's the way it happened. We looked at each other, and we both knew that we were meant to be together.'

She looked at Gray, half expecting his lip to be curled in disgust or disbelief, but he was just drinking his coffee, and in the darkness it was even harder than usual to read his expression.

'Mark manages one of the big orchestras,' she went on after a moment. 'We had lunch, supposedly to talk about an international tour we were organising, but we ended up talking about us, and then we had lunch the next day, and then dinner... There was something inevitable about it all. I couldn't help myself,' she said, as if pleading for his understanding. 'I'd never felt like that about anyone before. Mark was everything I'd ever wanted.' Her voice wavered and then steadied. 'I thought we were made for each other.'

'But he was married?'

Clare's shoulders slumped. 'Yes, he was married. Maybe I should have guessed, but I didn't. I was too happy to think,' she added sadly. 'When Mark told me, I was totally unprepared. It was such a shock. I felt...'

She turned her face away, unable to describe how she had felt. 'He said he loved me. He said that he and his wife had grown apart, but they had two small children. I couldn't be responsible for breaking up a family. We agreed that he should concentrate on trying to sort out his marriage and

we would be just good friends—just like you and Lizzy,'
she said. 'But, unlike you and Lizzy, I don't think it's possible to be just friends with someone you love.'

'Did you try?' asked Gray quietly.

'Oh, yes, we both tried, but I think we both knew it
wouldn't work. We still had to work together, but it was
agony seeing each other, loving each other, and knowing
it was hopeless. I'd almost decided to find a new job when
Pippa came back unexpectedly from Australia and then...
well, you know what happened then.

'The agency I work for is a small one, and my boss was
very kind. He suggested that I take some time off to give
myself time to get over everything. I think he must have
guessed about Mark, although we were always very discreet
in the office.

'I'm lucky,' Clare went on, trying to smile. 'He said that
he would keep my job for me and I thought that it would
be the best thing to do. It would give me a chance to try
and come to terms with Pippa's death and decide what best
to do for Alice...and to get used to not seeing Mark. I want
Mark to have a real chance to save his marriage.'

'And what about you?'

She lifted her shoulders in a hopeless gesture. 'I'm just
hoping that by the time I go home it won't hurt so much,'
she said honestly.

There was a long silence. 'I can see why you feel out of
place at Bushman's Creek,' said Gray at last. 'There's nothing that you want here.'

'There is one thing,' said Clare steadily. 'I want Alice to
be happy. I want that more than anything else, and I think
this will be the place she *is* happy.' She paused. 'I'm sorry
I was rude about the station this afternoon,' she apologised
a little awkwardly. 'It's not the place, it's just me. I'm not
used to it.'

'Alice will be,' he said. 'She's a Henderson. She'll grow up at Bushman's Creek, and this will be her home.'

Clare looked at him, wanting to believe him but not yet sure if she could. 'You seem very certain now that Jack will accept her.'

'I am. The more I see of her, the more I know that she's family.' Gray got to his feet. 'You should get some sleep. You may not feel at home in the outback, but you've worked hard today. I appreciate it,' he finished simply.

He held out a hand to help her to her feet, and Clare was so surprised that she took it without thinking. His fingers closed around hers, warm and strong, pulling her up easily, and she had to fight a sudden, desperate longing to cling to them.

'Th-thank you,' she said with an uncertain smile as he released her.

'Don't worry about Alice,' said Gray. 'She'll be fine. Jack and I will look after her and you'll be able to go home. Maybe things will work out for you and Mark after all.'

Standing on the dark verandah, with her hand still tingling from his touch, Clare couldn't help thinking that Mark had never seemed so far away. 'Maybe,' she said.

That conversation on the verandah marked a turning point for Clare. It was the beginning of a new relationship between her and Gray. He knew everything about her now, she realised, so she had no need to pretend. She just had to wait for Jack to return, and to push all thoughts of the past and the future from her mind.

It was easier than she had expected. The days at Bushman's Creek passed in a timeless rhythm. Clare cooked and cleaned and washed clothes and watered the plants on the verandah. It was a humdrum routine that once she would have despised, but sometimes, when she was

feeding the chickens or hanging nappies out on the line, she would forget that she had ever hankered after the challenge and stimulation of working in a busy office, or that she had ever spent her days juggling appointments and rushing from one meeting to another.

There were times when her life in London seemed very remote, like something that had happened to someone else. No phones rang frantically at Bushman's Creek, no messages flashed up on her computer screen demanding urgent attention. There was only the mournful cry of the rooks down by the creek, the whirring of insects as night fell, and the sound of Gray, stamping the dust from his boots on the verandah.

Sometimes Clare even forgot what she was doing there. No message came from Jack, and after the first couple of weeks she stopped asking Gray if he had heard anything from his brother. After a while, it didn't seem to matter that much. Alice had settled easily into her new routine. She adored Gray, and Clare was happy to share her care with him whenever he offered. She taught him how to bathe Alice, how to change her and burp her, how to sterilise her bottles and how to soothe her when she was upset. He even persevered with his attempts to feed his small niece, although it was the one area in which Alice absolutely refused to co-operate.

Gradually Clare let herself relax for the first time since Pippa's death. She felt closer to her sister at Bushman's Creek. She would never love the outback as Pippa had done, but it no longer appalled her as it had that first day, and as the days turned into weeks she found herself noticing things that she had been unable to appreciate at first— the fiery sunsets, the blur of pink as a flock of galahs took flight, and the gnarled beauty of the ghost gums, their silvery trunks sharply outlined in the crystalline light.

In the evenings, she would sit with Gray on the verandah and listen to the night. She learnt to recognise his deadpan sense of humour and the way his eyes crinkled when he was amused. He had an extraordinary capacity for stillness, and she would study him from under her lashes, intrigued by his self-containment.

Claire found herself thinking less and less about London, and more and more about Gray, about the kind of man he was, and the life he led. Sometimes she even let herself wonder whether he would ever look for another woman to share it with him at Bushman's Creek, but it was something she never quite dared to ask, and Gray himself never mentioned the subject at all.

CHAPTER FIVE

'ARE you busy?'

Clare put down the rolling pin and looked at Gray in surprise. 'Not desperately,' she said, brushing her floury hands on her apron. 'Why?'

'I need to talk to you about something.'

He had been preoccupied ever since he had come back from Mathison a couple of hours ago, and although he had handed over the groceries Clare had requested from the store, his replies to her attempts at conversation had been random, and he had disappeared almost immediately outside. And now he was back, looking even more guarded than usual.

A frown touched Clare's eyes. 'That sounds ominous,' she said as lightly as she could. 'Let me just put this in the fridge.' She put the pastry away, and took off her apron before turning back to Gray. 'What is it?'

'Let's go for a walk,' said Gray, avoiding a direct answer. 'The creek's nice at this time of day.'

Clare hesitated. 'Alice is asleep.'

'We needn't go far. And Joe's around. I asked him to fix that window, so he'll hear her if she cries.'

'All right.' Clare picked up the battered stockman's hat that Gray had insisted she wear. It was second nature now to put it on when she went outside, even if she was only going to feed the chooks.

So much that had seemed strange to her when she had arrived three weeks ago was now familiar, she thought as Gray held open the screen door for her and they walked

down the verandah steps together. She was used to the brilliance of the light, to the vast blue bowl of the sky, and the hot glare that struck her like a blow as soon as she emerged from the shade. She was used to the birds that exploded out of the trees over the waterhole, shrieking and squawking as they approached. She was even getting used to Gray, to his calm, quiet presence and the steadiness of his gaze.

Not to his smile, though. Clare didn't think she would ever get used to that. It caught her unawares every time, clogging the breath in her throat as the quiet mouth curled slowly upwards, and she would be held by the deepening crease in his cheek and the gleam of his white teeth and the lurking amusement in his eyes.

They walked through the hot, still silence along the creek bed. Dry leaves rustled beneath their feet and the sunlight through the stately gums threw fractured shade over them, shifting and flickering as they moved.

'I picked up the mail in Mathison this morning,' said Gray at last. 'There was a letter from Jack.'

'From *Jack*?' Stupidly, it was the last thing Clare had expected. She had forgotten about Jack, forgotten how desperately she had wanted to find Alice's father and let her start a new life with him. There was something dreamlike about the quiet creek. She had been content to walk beside Gray, aware as always of his steadiness and his strength, but not thinking of anything, just waiting until he was ready to say what he had to say, and now reality had intruded with sickening suddenness.

'What…what did he say?' she asked in a voice unlike her own.

'Just that he was feeling unsettled.' Gray stopped and turned to face her. 'He made a spur-of-the-moment decision to go and look at some bulls in Argentina instead of Texas,

and now he's down there he seems to have decided to stay for a while.'

'So he didn't get any of your messages?'

'No.'

There was a fallen tree nearby, its trunk worn smooth with age, and Clare sat down on it, feeling ridiculously shaken. After a moment, Gray sat beside her. He had an airmail envelope in his shirt pocket, and he took it out, pulling out the letter inside and scanning it as if hoping the contents would miraculously have changed since the last time he'd read it.

Clare made an effort to pull herself together. She ought to be glad Jack had got in touch at last, instead of wishing that his letter had never arrived. So what if it meant that she would have to start thinking about the future and the time when she would have to say goodbye to Alice and leave Bushman's Creek? It had been bound to happen some time, and perhaps the sooner the better.

'Has he given you an address where you can reach him now?' she asked, trying to sound practical.

Gray shook his head. 'He's gone travelling now. He doesn't even say where. All the letter says is that he feels as if he needs a complete break.' Beneath his hat, Clare saw him frown slightly as he refolded the letter. 'I know he couldn't have known that you would turn up with Alice, but it's not like Jack to do something like this.'

'Well...does he say when he'll be back?'

'Not until after the Wet, he says.'

'And when's that?'

He turned to look at her. 'Not for another five months, at least.'

'Five *months*!' Clare stared at him in dismay as the full implications of Jack's letter began to sink in. 'Five months...' she said again, more slowly.

'I'm sorry, Clare,' said Gray.

There was a long silence. Mindlessly, Clare picked up a gum leaf and crushed it between her fingers to release the smell, holding it to her nose as she breathed in its scent, so evocative of the dry, dusty landscape. She was very aware of the smooth wood beneath her thighs, of the corellas squabbling in the treetops, of Gray, sitting still and solid and somehow definite beside her.

'I'll have to go home,' she said dully, not looking at him. All that effort, all the strain of bringing Alice out to Australia and adjusting to a new life, all for nothing.

Gray hesitated. 'You could stay,' he offered carefully.

'Only for another two months.' Clare let the pieces of leaf scatter desolately on the ground. 'I've only got a three-month visa, and there's not much point if Jack won't be back before my time is up. I can't stay any longer even if I could afford it. You know how strict the immigration rules are.'

'Not if you're an Australian—or married to one.'

Clare sat very still, staring blindly at the fragments of leaf scattered around her dusty sandals until, very slowly, she lifted her head to stare at Gray with eyes that were clear and grey and wide with the dawning realisation of what he was suggesting.

'You could marry me,' he said.

Unable to speak, Clare could only sit there, stunned, while the silence around them seemed to twang with the echo of his words. *Marry me...marry me...marry me...*

Gray looked calmly back at her as if he had suggested nothing more momentous than an afternoon stroll. His brown eyes were perfectly steady, his expression quite unreadable.

Clare moistened her lips. '*Marry* you?' she croaked at last, suddenly convinced that she must have misheard.

'As my wife, you'd be entitled to stay in the country,' he pointed out.

'But…but…you don't want to marry me!'

Something flickered in the brown eyes, but was gone too quickly for Clare to identify it. 'I'm trying to think of a practical solution to the problem,' he said. 'It seems to me that Alice is the most important thing to consider. She's happy, and settled, and it would just disrupt her to take her all the way back to England and then return when Jack finally reappears, and you say you can't afford to do that anyway. I don't imagine you'd be prepared to leave her here, so we need to find some way for you to stay until Jack comes back, and the easiest is for you to marry an Australian. That might as well be me.

'I don't see any reason why we shouldn't come to an agreement,' Gray went on, when it was obvious that Clare was still struggling to absorb the idea. 'I'm not suggesting that we stay married for ever. As soon as Jack returns and Alice's future is settled we can agree to separate, and you can go back to your job in England as you'd planned.'

'I…I don't know,' Clare stammered. Her head was whirling at the very thought of marrying Gray, and she laid her hands flat on the wood either side of her to steady herself.

Gray was leaning forward, his arms resting on his thighs and his hands clasped loosely between his knees. His hat shaded his face, and he glanced up at Clare from beneath its dusty brim. 'What's the problem?' he asked.

Clare looked back at him a bit helplessly. 'Everything, really… I can't believe it would really be as easy as that to just get married and then divorced whenever it suited us.'

'I don't see why not,' said Gray. 'We'd both understand

that it was just a practical arrangement. It won't be very romantic, but then it doesn't need to be.'

No, it wouldn't be romantic. Clare let herself think about Mark, and how she had once dreamt of marrying him. How could she have known that she would end up thinking seriously about marrying a man as different from Mark as could be imagined, and for such very different reasons?

She tried to consider the matter dispassionately. Marriage to Gray would solve her visa problem and enable her to stay with Alice as long as she was needed. That was the most important thing. And yet...*could* it be that easy? She looked at him from under her lashes. What would it be like, being married to Gray? Would he just carry on as now, treating her as a cross between a housekeeper and a guest, or would he treat her as a wife? A slow shudder made its way down her spine at the thought, and she averted her gaze.

Tracing an invisible pattern on the log with one finger, she asked, 'What about Lizzy?'

'What about her?' he said slowly.

'You're still in love with her.'

Gray turned his head and looked into her face, an enigmatic expression in his brown eyes. 'Am I?'

There was a long pause, and in the end it was Clare who looked away. 'What if she changes her mind about you and then finds out that you're married?'

'That's not going to happen,' he said flatly. 'Lizzy's engaged to someone she met in Perth. She won't be coming home now.'

His expression told her nothing, but Clare wondered if he was more hurt than he wanted to admit by Lizzy's engagement, and it occurred to her for the first time that he might have reasons of his own for this strange marriage he was proposing. Perhaps a wife of his own, however tem-

porary, might salve his pride and help him put a good face on Lizzy's wedding.

Clare wasn't sure whether the thought made her feel better or worse. 'I see,' she said slowly.

'Lizzy's not concerned in this. It just happens that neither of us are in a position to marry the people we wanted to marry, and neither of us will expect anything out of this marriage other than a practical solution to a practical problem.'

'Yes, but the problem is mine,' Clare felt obliged to point out. 'Why should you be prepared to marry a woman you hardly know?'

'Because of Alice,' said Gray simply. 'She's family, and the Hendersons look after their own. I think it would be best for her if you stayed until Jack gets back, and if marrying you is the only way that can happen, that's what I'll do. It would solve the immediate problem of someone to look after her during the day, too. If you weren't here, I'd have to hire someone else, and good housekeepers are hard to find.'

'You mean you'd really get married for the sake of a clean house and regular meals on the table?' said Clare a little bitterly.

'No,' he said, looking straight into her eyes. 'But I would for Alice. It's not as if it would be for ever. I know you're not in love with me, any more than I'm in love with you, and there's no point in either of us pretending that we are. You don't have to pretend to like Bushman's Creek, either. I know it's not your kind of place, but London will still be waiting for you when Jack comes home. It'll only be for a few months, and you said yourself that you wanted to stay away for a while. Why not stay here, with Alice?'

Why not? thought Clare. 'It would be much cheaper than travelling,' she said, almost to herself. 'And it would mean

I don't need to leave as soon as Jack gets back. I could make sure Alice has a chance to get used to someone else looking after her— Oh, this is ridiculous!' She leapt to her feet as the absurdity of the situation struck her. 'I can't believe that I'm actually *thinking* about marrying a man I haven't even—'

She stopped abruptly, as if she had been brought up short at the very edge of a chasm.

'Haven't even kissed?' Gray finished for her. He rose so that he could look down into Clare's face. 'Is that what you were going to say?'

Her breath leaked away at the realisation of how disturbingly close he was. 'Yes,' she said on a gasp, wanting to sound cool and composed and unperturbed, but acutely conscious instead of his nearness and of her heart booming thunderously in her chest.

'That's easily remedied, isn't it?'

Clare didn't—couldn't—answer. She could only stand there, held by the light in his eyes, while somewhere deep inside her a mixture of anticipation and horror at the strength of her treacherous longing shivered into life.

Without haste, Gray took off her hat and dropped it onto the log where they had been sitting. Then, very deliberately, he took off his own. He held it in one hand, and with the other reached out to caress her cheek before his fingers slid slowly beneath the dark, silky hair.

Clare could feel them, warm and strong, at the nape of her neck. Trembling, she let him pull her unresisting towards him, and her hands went up instinctively to rest against his chest for support. For a long, long moment, Gray examined her face, his eyes alight with an expression that made her hammering heart falter, and then his mouth came down on hers.

The creek bed dropped away beneath Clare's feet and

she closed her eyes, half-thrilled and half-terrified by the intensity of her reaction to the first touch of his lips. It was as if a shaft of sun had pierced the shade and drenched her in dazzling light that reduced the world around her to a faint blur and left her aware only of Gray, of the warmth of his hand and the taste of his mouth and the feel of his lips exploring hers with such gentle, devastating effect.

Her fingers curled into the material of his shirt for support, and she leant into him, instinctively seeking the hard security of his body as a bulwark against the alarming knowledge of how easily the sensations spilling through her could spin her out of control.

Still holding his hat in his hand, Gray's arm went round her and he pulled her closer against him as he deepened the kiss. Clare melted into him. She was boneless, dizzy with delight, helpless beneath the teasing, tantalising persuasion of his lips, and when Gray lifted his head she murmured an unthinking protest.

His hold on her tightened for a moment in response before he released her reluctantly. 'Think about marrying me now,' he said.

Clare looked dazedly at him, unaware of how huge and dark her eyes were, or how invitingly her mouth trembled. She felt suspended, somehow disembodied and unable to move, while her senses sang with the remembered feel of Gray's kiss, and she was suddenly, intensely aware of her surroundings. There was silence in the creek, hot and still and laced with the scent of dust and bark and dry leaves. Clare could feel it beating around her, could sense the dazzling light beyond the shade and the movement of the earth beneath her feet.

And then the branches above her head erupted into life as a flock of galahs rose shrieking and squabbling in the air, and the spell was broken. Abruptly aware that her legs

wouldn't hold her, Clare dropped onto the log and shook her head to clear it.

Gray misinterpreted the gesture. 'You don't need to make up your mind immediately,' he said.

'I didn't mean that I was saying no,' said Clare, making a stupendous effort to pull herself together. 'I meant... I'm not sure what I meant,' she confessed helplessly, even as she wondered what on earth was the matter with her.

Wasn't she Clare, calm, sensible, level-headed Clare, famous in the office for her composure and her ability to keep her head in a crisis? It had only been a kiss, not even a long or particularly passionate one, she reminded herself. There was no reason for her to feel as if the world was still reeling crazily around her.

'I'll have to think about it,' she said.

'Of course.' Gray's eyes rested on her flushed face as he settled his hat calmly back on his head. 'Take as long as you want. I need to get back,' he added after a moment, and when Clare said nothing he turned to go, making his way back along the creek.

'When you've thought about it,' he said as he left, 'let me know.'

Clare stood by the cot that Joe had painstakingly restored to its former glory. With a new mattress it was perfect. She ran her hand along the smooth edge, wishing that Alice wasn't sleeping quite so peacefully, longing to pick her up and cuddle her. Sometimes, like now, when she looked at Pippa's daughter, she loved her so much that it hurt. She would do anything for her.

Even if it meant marrying Gray Henderson.

She hadn't, in the end, had to think about it for very long. If there had been an alternative, Clare would have taken it, but there wasn't. The rules said that she could only

spend three months in Australia, and she couldn't afford to leave and come back on a new visa, even if she could be sure that the authorities would let her in. No, marriage was her only option, and Gray her only possible husband.

Clare wasn't sure why the idea of marrying him made her so nervous. It wasn't as if he were unpleasant or unattractive. With sudden insight, she wondered whether it might not be easier if he were.

The memory of his kiss shivered down her spine. If only he hadn't kissed her. If only she didn't clench with deep, dangerous thrill whenever she thought about how it had felt to kiss him back.

Confused by her own reaction, Clare had tossed and turned all night. Surely it couldn't be right to kiss like that when they were both in love with someone else? Surely it shouldn't have felt like that? Gray hadn't admitted it in so many words, but he was obviously still in love with Lizzy. And then there was Mark—Mark whom she had loved so desperately. She had been so sure that there would never be anybody else.

But when she tried to conjure up Mark's face, all Clare could see was Gray standing before her, the brim of his hat shading his face and that maddeningly elusive smile bracketing his quiet mouth. Gray, with his unfathomable brown eyes and his slow, easy stride and his lean, hard body.

The man she was going to marry.

Clare stood looking down into the cot for a long time before she took a deep breath and went to find Gray.

He was on the verandah, where she had expected him to be, leaning on the rail and looking out at the stars that speckled the night sky above the creek. Clare could make out his still figure, but when he turned his head at her approach, his features were indistinct. She had been stupidly nervous about what she was going to say, but she was glad

now that she hadn't decided to wait until the morning. This was going to be the kind of conversation that it was easier to have in the dark.

She went to lean next to him on the rail, and for a while they watched the stars together without speaking. It was very quiet and blissfully cool after the heat of the day, and as the peace of the night settled around her, Clare felt her doubts fade.

'I've been thinking about what you said yesterday,' she said at last, without taking her eyes from the sky.

'About marrying me?'

'Yes.' She hesitated. 'Is the offer still open?'

Gray turned to look at her face, pale and luminous in the starlight. 'Yes,' he said.

'Then I'd like to accept.' She rushed on so that he would know that she didn't expect him to sweep her into his arms or pretend a delight he didn't feel. 'I know that it's not the way either of us would have wanted to be getting married, but, as you said, it's not as if it's for ever, and it's worth it for Alice.'

Uncomfortably aware that she was rattling, Clare forced herself to stop and draw breath. 'I do have one proviso, though.'

Gray stilled. 'What is it?'

'I think we should draw up a legal agreement before the marriage to make it clear that I have no claim on you or your property when we part. I don't want there to be any question of me benefiting financially from marrying you. You certainly won't be getting any financial advantage out of me,' she added ruefully. 'I don't have any assets.'

'I wouldn't say that,' he said slowly, his eyes on her face.

For some reason, Clare felt herself blushing. 'Apart from

my prowess with a dustpan and brush, of course,' she said with a quick, nervous smile.

'That wasn't quite what I was thinking of.' Gray turned back to face the shadowy outline of the gums against the dark sky. 'We can draw up a legal agreement if you think it's necessary. I'll speak to my lawyer about it, and maybe we could take a trip to Perth some time to sign it. It might not be a bad idea to go to Perth anyway,' he went on reflectively. 'You'll want to buy a wedding dress, and we can get the ring and anything else you and Alice will need if you're going to stay here a while.'

'Do you think it's necessary to spend money on things like a wedding dress?' said Clare, sounding doubtful. 'It's not as if it will be a wedding in the real sense.'

'You know that and I know that, but as far as everybody else is concerned it's got to be absolutely convincing. The immigration authorities are much more likely to question our marriage if we don't have a proper wedding, with a dress and photographs and guests. We'll need to invite everyone in the district and make a show, I'm afraid.'

'I hadn't thought about other people being involved,' she confessed. 'Won't they all think it's a bit odd, you suddenly deciding to marry me?'

The corner of his mouth lifted. 'I don't think they'll be surprised. By the time we get married you'll have been here nearly two months, and we'll have been living alone together in the homestead all that time. What could be more natural than that we should fall in love?'

A wave of colour surged up Clare's cheeks, and she was passionately grateful for the darkness. 'I suppose they're not to know how we really feel,' she agreed stiffly after a moment.

'No, and they have to carry on not knowing,' said Gray. 'You've seen how many people pass through the station for

one reason or another, and we can't afford to let anyone suspect that it's not in fact a real marriage. We're going to have to keep up the pretence the whole time. Do you think you can do that?'

'I can if you can,' she said, only to be assailed by sudden doubt. 'At least…'

'What?'

'Nothing,' she said quickly.

'Tell me,' said Gray, straightening from the rail to frown down at her.

'It's just…well, there is one thing…' Unable to look at him directly, Clare fixed her eyes on her finger, that was apparently preoccupied with drawing a meandering pattern on the rail, and wondered how to ask him whether he wanted to sleep with her or not.

It was stupid to be embarrassed about it, she scolded herself. They were both grown up. Taking an uneven breath, she launched into speech before she had time to change her mind. 'I wondered what you thought…whether you were thinking that you…that *we*…' Oh, this was hopeless! Clare made herself stop and start again. 'I suppose I'm trying to ask you exactly how married we're going to be.' She glanced at Gray. 'You know what I mean!'

'Yes, I know what you mean,' he said. Reaching out, he tucked a strand of hair thoughtfully behind Clare's ear. 'How married would you like to be, Clare?'

'I…I'm not sure,' she confessed.

'Then we'll wait until you are,' he said calmly. 'It's up to you.'

'But what if it was up to you?'

A smile hovered around his mouth as he looked down into her face. 'I'm a man, Clare, not a machine, and you're an attractive woman. If we're going to make the marriage look convincing, we'll have to share a bedroom, and, in the

circumstances, it seems to me that we might as well make the most of things.' He shrugged slightly. 'There's no hurry to decide. Why don't you think about it?'

'I don't want to think about it.' Clare turned to face him. 'I'm tired of thinking,' she told him, her mind made up. 'We're going to get married, and it'll be easier for us both if we could be as normal as possible. We're both adults, and neither of us has other commitments. There's no reason why we shouldn't…you know…'

'I know,' said Gray gravely, although Clare was sure she could detect amusement lurking in his voice.

She steeled herself to continue. 'I mean, it's awkward discussing it in cold blood, but maybe we could do what normal people do. We could try and forget that we're doing this for Alice, and just…get to know each other.'

Gray's smile gleamed in the dim light as he put his strong hands to her waist and pulled her gently towards him. 'Like this?' he suggested.

'Yes,' said Clare, drawing an uneven breath. This was what her words had invited, what she had wanted, but she was still unprepared for the jolt of reaction at the feel of his hard hands through the thin material of her dress, or the quick pulse of excitement running beneath her skin. 'We could…pretend…that we're falling in love and…and see where it leads us,' she said, her voice growing ragged as Gray bent his head until his lips were almost—but not quite—touching hers.

'Let's pretend now,' he said, and closed the last unbearable gap between them.

Clare let out a sigh, parting her lips beneath his and sliding her arms around his neck, abandoning herself to the intoxicating pleasure of his mouth exploring hers, of his slow, sure hands moulding her against him. Adrift in a swirl of sensation, she felt liquefied, her bones dissolved into

honey, and she clung to him, bewitched by the enchantment of the kiss that had them both in thrall. It was as if it had a will of its own, so that neither could have broken free, even if they had wanted to.

She never knew how long they kissed there on the dark verandah. She knew only that the kiss seemed to last for ever, and yet ended much, much too soon. Gray's hands came up to cup her face between his long, strong fingers and he eased himself away from her, letting her down gradually with softer and softer kisses until, with one final brief kiss on her lips, he managed to lift his head and they looked at each other for a long, breathless moment.

Clare managed a shaky smile. 'If I were pretending to fall in love with you, I'd tell you that I'd been thinking about that ever since you kissed me in the creek yesterday,' she said unsteadily.

'And if I were pretending,' Gray replied with a twisted smile, 'I'd tell you I'd been thinking about it a lot longer than that.'

She looked at him uncertainly. They were just pretending…weren't they?

'Come on,' he said as he released her, 'I'll see you to your room.'

That set the pattern for the next few days. During the day, Gray treated her as he had always done. Clare was just a housekeeper, and he was just a station owner, and none of the stockmen could have guessed that when they went back to their quarters after the evening meal Gray would take her hand and lead her out onto the verandah and kiss her in the starlight.

Clare told herself that they were just doing what they had agreed. They were just getting to know each other, pretending to be a normal couple so that they could pretend to have a normal marriage, but she felt increasingly twitchy

as the days passed. The strength of her response to Gray's slightest touch unsettled her. She couldn't stop thinking about him, about his mouth and his hands and the unyielding masculinity of his body.

Sometimes she would look at Gray, and the memory of his kisses would swamp her, leaving her giddy and breathless with desire. Of course, it was just a physical thing, Clare knew that, but it kept her jittery and on edge, unable to concentrate on anything except the shiver of anticipation as darkness fell. She longed for the moment when Gray pulled her down onto his lap, although every time a voice deep inside her warned how easy it would be to forget that it was just as an artificial exercise.

Gray never forgot. It was always he who put an end to their kisses. To Clare's piercing disappointment, he would tip her out of his lap and escort her politely back to her room. If they were a real couple, she thought in frustration, he wouldn't leave her at her door with a chaste goodnight.

'It's up to you,' Gray had said. His words echoed in Clare's mind as she hung out the washing and scattered scraps for the chooks. All she had to do was tell him, she realised slowly. It wasn't as if they had to make a big deal out of it. They were both free, both there, both committed to spending the next few months together. Why *shouldn't* they give in to the physical attraction between them? It didn't have to mean anything, Clare reasoned. They would just be making the most of an otherwise awkward situation.

She rehearsed all sorts of ways to tell Gray that she had made up her mind. It seemed terribly important to make it clear that as far as she was concerned it was a purely physical issue. She would tell him that he had no need to worry about her getting involved, that it would only be a temporary affair and that she had no expectations of him.

But the moment Gray took Clare in his arms that night,

all her careful arguments vanished, forgotten in the shivery, spiralling excitement that gripped her. How could she talk when his lips were on hers, when his hand was sliding over her thigh beneath her skirt, warm and insistent against her bare flesh? How could she think when he was pressing slow, sure, seductive kisses along the curve of her throat?

'We'd better stop while we still can,' he murmured reluctantly as she tipped her head back, unable to prevent a tiny moan of pleasure escaping her.

'No,' she gasped. All those fine speeches she had prepared in her head, and 'no' was all she could say! 'No...don't stop,' she said breathlessly. 'I don't want to stop.'

Gray's hands stilled against her, and he lifted his head to look wordlessly into her face before abruptly putting her off his lap and getting to his feet. Dismay trickled down Clare's spine. Didn't he want her? Was he going to reject her after all? Did he think it was better to wait until they knew each other better?

She braced herself for a kind, tactful speech, but when Gray took her hand and led her down the dark corridor he didn't stop outside the room where Alice was sleeping, where always before he had stopped to say goodnight, but pulled her instead into his bedroom.

Dizzy with relief, Clare hardly realised when he stopped just inside the door and let her go. It was dark in the room and she couldn't make out his expression clearly, but there was a new note of urgency in his voice.

'Are you sure, Clare?' he said.

She was trembling with anticipation, her heartbeat thumping along her veins and booming in her ears, and she smiled rather shakily. Lifting her hands, she laid them flat against his broad chest and thrilled as she felt his muscles flex in response. 'I'm sure,' she said softly.

Gray looked down into her shining eyes for a long moment, and then his slow smile gleamed in the darkness. 'Good,' he said, in a voice that vibrated over her skin, and he reached behind her to close the door with a soft click.

CHAPTER SIX

THEY left for Perth a week later. It felt very strange to be back in a city, thought Clare, marvelling at the cars and the shops and the gleaming office buildings soaring into the sky. It was all so *busy*. The pavements were crowded with smartly dressed people and the streets had a lively, cosmopolitan feel a world away from the stillness and silence of Bushman's Creek.

It should have been familiar, but somehow it wasn't. 'Familiar' now meant the homestead and the creek and the huge, dusty paddocks, and although Clare knew that Gray thought she was thrilled to be going back to a city, she hadn't been anxious to leave.

The last few days had been golden ones, and the nights long and sweet. Even wanting him as she had, Clare had been unprepared for the heart-stopping passion that had blazed between them when Gray reached for her that first night, and every night since she had been left awed and shaken by the intensity of her response to his touch and his taste and the feel of his taut, unyielding body, of his lips against her skin.

It grew harder and harder to remember that they were only pretending to be a normal couple. Only two days ago, Clare had come back from Mathison to find Gray attempting to give Alice lunch in the kitchen. She had driven into the town once before, to restock the store cupboard and buy some of the fresh fruit and vegetables they were unable to grow themselves, but the round trip took more than four hours, and she had left Alice in Gray's charge.

Last time Alice had been good as gold, but as soon as Clare had walked through the door she'd seen that she was playing up. The kitchen had been in a state of chaos, the mess on the floor around the highchair bearing witness to some nasty tantrums, and Gray's smile as he'd tried to persuade a mutinous Alice to accept another spoonful of the purée Clare had made for her had been what could only be described as fixed.

Sensing Clare's presence, he'd looked round to see her smiling in the doorway, holding a box of groceries balanced on her hip. She'd been dressed plainly but practically, in jeans and a soft blue shirt, and she'd looked quite different from the smart, strained woman who had waited for him on the hotel verandah in Mathison. The swing of dark hair had been pushed anyhow behind her ears and the huge, silvery-grey eyes had been alight with amusement.

At the sight of her, relief and something more had flitted across his face, but before Clare had had a chance to wonder what it meant, Alice had spotted her and burst into voluble if incomprehensible speech. Gray, she'd seemed to be saying, had absolutely no idea of how she liked to eat. She had waved her spoon imperiously to prove her point, sending a gob of puréed potato and carrot flying. More by luck than science, it had landed smack in the middle of Gray's face.

Gray had sighed, and wiped it from beneath his eye.

Laughing at his grimace, Clare had put down the box and gone over to wet a clean cloth at the sink.

'It's a very funny thing how a man who can jump from a galloping horse and wrestle a bull to the ground can't manage one small baby!' she teased him, as she bent to clean Alice's sticky face and hands, ignoring her vigorous protests.

'I don't know how you manage to get anything down her at all,' said Gray, resigned to his inadequacy.

'She likes to feed herself. I let her get on with it and clean up the mess afterwards,' Clare told him. Straightening, she saw that there was still a smear of purée on his cheek, and unthinkingly she laid a hand on his shoulder and wiped the mess away with a clean corner of the cloth. It was only when she made to draw back that she realised how easily she had touched him. She had cleaned him up as if he were a child, but as she glanced down into his eyes, there was nothing childlike about the way her heart lurched.

The look locked and held. It was as if there was an invisible force tugging between them, too strong to resist. Clare didn't even try. Her fingers tightened on his shoulder and she bent her head slowly to touch her lips to his. They kissed gently at first, but when she made to draw away Gray's arm came up to pull her down onto his knee. Clare sank against him, unresisting, her arms sliding around his neck as their kisses deepened hungrily.

Alice was not impressed. Outraged at the comprehensive loss of attention, she let out a piercing yell. Gray opened one eye and scowled at her, at which Alice shouted again and smacked the table, overturning her plastic dish. Vaguely becoming aware of her antics at last, Clare lifted her head reluctantly.

Satisfied that they were both now looking at *her*, Alice beamed at them, and as a reward for their obedience put her dish on her head as a hat.

'Alice!' Clare leapt up to grab it, and the moment passed. Nothing was said, but she felt that it had been an important step. It was the first time they had kissed like lovers during the day, and it had felt completely natural.

No, Clare hadn't been anxious to leave Bushman's Creek at all.

She studied Gray from under her lashes. By rights, he should have looked awkward and out of place against the sophisticated background of Perth, but somehow he didn't. He looked just as calm and assured as he did in the outback, and was driving the car they had hired at the airport with exactly the same easy competence as he swung onto a horse or flew a plane

Her eyes drifted reminiscently from his mouth down to rest on the long, strong, brown hands that rested with calm control on the steering wheel. She only had to look at his hands now and her skin would prickle with memory. She knew just how skilful they were, how strong and sure they felt against her body. She knew the deftness of his fingers as he undressed her, the intoxicating pleasure of his slow, slow kisses, the way he smiled as he rolled her beneath him. It gave her a secret thrill to watch him discussing a muster, or working in the yards, or checking in their bags for the flight down to Perth that morning, and to know that when night fell he was hers. Clare's mouth curved upwards in a smile of delicious anticipation.

Glancing at her, Gray saw her smile. 'Happy to be back in the city?'

Clare was oddly startled by his question. She had become so accustomed to her misery over Mark, her terrible grief for Pippa and the worry about what best to do for Alice, that it was with a sense of shock that she realised that she *was* happy, for the first time in a long while.

'Yes,' she said slowly.

Gray thought that it was because she was a city girl, back in a familiar environment, but it was more than that. It was because Alice, strapped securely into a car seat behind her, was cooing contentedly to herself as she tried to grab hold

of her toes. It was because the sky was blue and the air was sparkling and she could sense the ocean nearby.

It was because Gray was beside her, his eyes creased in the quiet smile that made her heart turn over, and they had the next three days together to forget about the future and everything that needed to be done at Bushman's Creek, and pretend instead that they were a normal family having a normal holiday. Three days in a beautiful city, three nights in a wide hotel bed, with Gray's lips and Gray's hands and Gray's lean, hard body.

Clare's smile widened and she settled luxuriously back into the car seat as she gazed out at the passing city scene. 'Yes,' she said again, 'I am.'

Gray had booked them into a hotel with views over the Swan River. From their room, Clare could see yachts sailing on the glittering blue water, and she exclaimed with pleasure as Gray joined her by the window.

She turned to him impulsively. 'This is wonderful!'

Her face was alight, her grey eyes shining. Gray looked away. 'I thought you'd like it,' he said, an odd note in his voice. 'Alice is sound asleep,' he added after a moment.

'I'm not surprised.' Clare went to lean over the cot the hotel had provided in a corner of the room. Alice was splayed out on her back, utterly relaxed. Her arms were above her head, her hands curled into tiny fists. 'She didn't sleep at all on the plane,' she went on, rejoining Gray at the window. 'I don't think we'll be going anywhere for a couple of hours.'

'No.'

For some reason, the air tightened. They glanced at each other, then away. Silence stretched between them, shimmering with possibility. Clare could feel a trembling begin deep inside her, and when at last Gray lifted his hand to

smooth a stray hair away from her cheek, she caught her breath.

'So what shall we do until she wakes up?' he asked softly.

Clare's heart was thudding with slow, painful insistence against her ribs. Her skin had contracted at the graze of his fingers on her face and all her senses had snarled into a tight knot of desire. Gray had never looked at her like this before, in the bright afternoon light, and her mouth dried at the expression in his eyes.

'What do you suggest?' she said in a husky voice.

'We-ell,' said Gray, letting his hand drift down her throat, 'I've got a lot of business calls to make. You could look at a guidebook and decide what you want to see.'

His fingers had reached the collar of her blouse. Now they were slipping beneath it to stroke her collarbone, a featherlight caress that set Clare's body thrumming. 'I could,' she said with difficulty, hardly able to hear herself over the pulse booming in her ears.

'Or...'

'Yes?' breathed Clare as Gray's other hand came up and he began to unfasten the buttons of her shirt with a tantalising lack of haste.

'Or we could lie down,' he suggested, a smile lurking around his mouth.

An answering smile trembled on Clare's lips. 'Are you tired?'

'No.'

The last button fell apart. Very deliberately, Gray slid the blouse from her shoulders and let it fall unheeded to the floor. He put his hands to Clare's waist, his smile deepening as she was unable to prevent a sharp intake of breath, and she quivered, her eyes darkening in helpless response

as he caressed the satiny warmth of her skin with his thumbs.

'Are you?' he asked.

'No,' whispered Clare as she succumbed to temptation and slid her hands up to his shoulders, savouring the feel of his lean strength. 'Not at all.'

Afterwards, long afterwards, she opened her eyes. High above the ground as they were, they hadn't bothered to pull the curtains, and the late afternoon sunlight was pouring through the window and onto the bed where they lay entwined.

Clare felt as if she were drenched in its golden light, and she stretched luxuriously, turning her face to press a kiss against Gray's warm, sleek shoulder.

'It's just as well Alice sleeps so soundly,' murmured Gray, and she lifted her head to find him watching her, his brown eyes amused and warmer than she had ever seen them before.

He looked so relaxed that Clare was conscious of something uncoiling inside her, a feeling that began to unravel at an alarming rate. She didn't want to know what it meant. Knowing would mean that she had to do something about it, and all she wanted was to lie there with Gray and hold onto the moment as long as she could.

'*Is* she still asleep?' she asked lazily, spreading her hand over his chest and feeling its steady rise and fall.

'Amazingly enough,' said Gray. He wound a lock of her hair around one finger and gave it a teasing tug. 'We weren't exactly quiet.'

Clare laughed and blushed. 'We won't be able to do that when she's older!'

There was a tiny pause. Clare heard her own words, with their easy assumption that they would still be making love when Alice was old enough to notice what they were doing,

and she bit her lip. She wouldn't be there when Alice was older. The reminder was like a cloud passing over the sun, blotting out its warmth and light.

Pulling her hand away from him, she sat up.

'What is it?'

'Nothing.' Clare had her back to Gray so that he couldn't see her face. 'I was just getting a little carried away, that's all,' she said with determined brightness.

'What do you mean?' There was a faint frown in his voice.

'I forgot for a moment that I won't be here when Alice is older.'

Behind her, Clare could hear him throw back the sheet and get out of bed. 'No, you'll be going back to London, won't you?' he said expressionlessly.

'Yes.' Desperately trying to inject some enthusiasm into her voice at the prospect, she tried again. 'Yes, I will.'

She got up, too, and found her robe in the case, wrapping it tightly around her as if seeking comfort. Of course she would be going back to London. That was where she belonged, where her real life was. She had never intended her time in Australia to be more than temporary. In a few months' time, Clare reminded herself, she would go home, and she would remember Gray with gratitude for making it easier to leave Alice in a loving home. He had helped her to get over Mark, too, she realised now. She owed him a lot.

'Gray?' Turning, she saw that he had pulled on his trousers and was shrugging back into his shirt. His face, when he glanced across the bed at her, was shuttered, his eyes impenetrable.

'What?'

'I wanted to say…' Faced with his cool indifference, the words died on Clare's lips.

Gray was doing up the buttons on his shirt. 'You don't need to say anything, Clare,' he said curtly. 'We both know exactly what the situation is.'

'I know. I just don't want you thinking that I'm....that I'm taking it seriously.'

'Taking what seriously? The sex?'

'Yes.' She swallowed. It sounded so impersonal when he put it like that. 'What we have is great, but I know it's only temporary. That might even be part of its attraction, I think,' she added hesitantly. 'I suppose what I'm trying to say is that you don't need to worry about me get-ting...emotionally involved.' Faint colour stained her cheeks as she thought about how she clung to him, the unthinking endearments that tumbled from her lips as he made love to her. 'I know it must seem sometimes as if—'

'It doesn't seem anything,' Gray interrupted her harshly, shoving his shirt into his trousers. 'Look, Clare, we came to an agreement. You don't need to apologise for enjoying it.'

'I'm not! I just—'

'I don't see the point in discussing it,' he went on in a flat voice. 'We agreed to make the most of things, and that's what we're doing, but when Jack returns we'll go back to our old lives. That's what we both want, isn't it?'

'Yes, that's what we want,' agreed Clare dully. There was a heavy silence, and then she turned away to find her washbag. 'Excuse me, I think I'll have a shower.'

She stood under the streaming water and told herself it *was* what she wanted. She hated the idea that Gray might think she was going to do something stupid like fall in love with him, so why should she feel depressed because he had made it abundantly clear that he was in absolutely no dan-ger of falling in love with her? As far as he was concerned, theirs was a purely physical relationship, and that was good,

Clare told herself hastily. It would make it so much easier to say goodbye when the time came. By then she would probably be glad to go.

Later, when Alice was awake, they took her out and bought her a pushchair. Clare had been worried that Alice, used to being carried around, might object to her new mode of transport, but she settled into it without protest. Pushing her through the streets was certainly easier on the arms, Clare thought gratefully. Alice was growing all the time, and she soon got heavy.

The shops were closing as they left the store and strolled back to the hotel. The streets were crowded, and the pavement cafés full of tourists resting tired feet and office workers enjoying a drink at the end of the day. Clare loved the vibrant atmosphere. It reminded her of what she had been missing at Bushman's Creek. She looked at the laughing groups around the café tables and remembered how she had used to go for a drink with colleagues after work, to gossip over the day or discuss whether to go to a film or out for a meal. Perth was very different from London, but it had the same cosmopolitan buzz, and Clare absorbed its invigorating energy as she walked through the streets. She felt taller, more confident, more like herself with every step.

'This is my kind of place,' she told Gray. 'It's a pity we can't stay longer.'

'There's nothing to stop you coming back when you leave Bushman's Creek,' he replied in a cool voice. 'You could spend a few days here before you get the plane back to London. I've got friends here who would be glad to show you around.'

'What, even though they'll think I'll be leaving you after only a couple of months of marriage?' she said tightly, her hands tightening on the handles of the pushchair. Anyone

would think that he was counting the days until he would see the back of her!

Gray shrugged. 'It won't matter then. Once Jack's back we can tell everyone the truth, and you can go home.'

The hotel offered a baby-listening service, and they opted to eat in one of its restaurants so that they could get back to Alice quickly if she woke to find herself in a strange room. Having looked at the menu, and gulped at the prices, Clare was glad that she had brought her best dress with her, and she spent a long time in the bathroom getting ready that night.

There was a new distance between her and Gray, and Clare didn't know whether to welcome it or resent it. It had been too easy to slip into intimacy at Bushman's Creek, and perhaps this trip to Perth was just what they both needed to remember how different they really were. Gray was making it very clear that their relationship would be over the minute Jack returned to the station, and, to Clare, his comments seemed designed to remind her that she didn't belong at Bushman's Creek and never would.

It was no use pretending that she *did* belong, Clare told herself as she applied mascara carefully to her lashes. The Clare who spent her days happily cooking and cleaning at Bushman's Creek was an aberration.

That Clare wore the oldest clothes she had and barely glanced in a mirror. She sang as she brushed the endless dust off the verandah, and watered the vegetable plot, and picked lemons fresh from the tree. She hung the washing out to dry crisp as a board in the heat, and for entertainment she carried Alice out to the shady creek to watch the birds swooping and diving over the waterhole. That was the Clare who could be so easily beguiled into forgetting the agreement she had made with Gray, into letting herself believe that she would be happy to spend her whole life at

Bushman's Creek, the Clare who would need only the tiniest push to fall hopelessly, desperately in love with him.

But that wasn't the real Clare, she reminded herself almost fiercely as she studied her reflection in the bathroom mirror. Her dress was simple and elegant, relieved from dullness by its colour, a deep, vivid jade. It was a classic tailored look, not very adventurous, perhaps, but the one that suited her best. She looked serene, poised, capable, the kind of woman who had her life completely under control, the kind of woman she *was*.

'That's the real me,' Clare said to her reflection.

She had accentuated her eyes just as she had always done in the past. The deep red lipstick was one she always wore, knowing how well it suited her pale skin and dark hair. So why did she look so unfamiliar? It was as if she were wearing someone else's face.

No, Clare told herself, that's me. I always look like this when I go out in the evenings. I always wear make-up. I always dress smartly. I'm not that other Clare, with her dreamy smile and her hair pushed anyhow behind her ears. I can enjoy being her for a few months with Gray, but that's not who I really am. I'm smart, sensible, city Clare, and I'd better not forget it.

Picking up her bag, she turned abruptly for the door. Her high-heeled shoes felt peculiar now, too, and she leant against the frame while she adjusted them more comfortably, first on one foot and then the other.

Gray had been standing by the window, his hands in his pockets, looking out at the city lights with a preoccupied frown. The sound of the bathroom door opening at last made him turn, and he saw her balancing on one foot, a hand against the doorframe to steady her while she eased a finger between her heel and the narrow strap of the shoe.

Then she put her foot to the floor and walked forward,

and it was as if a completely different woman had come out of the bathroom. She was stunning, with brilliant eyes and a vivid, sultry mouth. Gray's jaw tightened as his eyes travelled from the smooth, dark hair to the dress that lovingly hugged the contours of her body and down over slender knees to the elegant, strappy shoes.

'You look very…smart,' he said.

Smart. He made it sound like an insult. Clare wouldn't have minded if he had said anything else—beautiful, elegant, sophisticated, glamorous, even *nice* would have done!—but 'smart' was such a hard, cold word, a word that was the antithesis of everything at Bushman's Creek.

'It looked like an expensive restaurant,' she said, tight-lipped. 'I thought it would be worth making an effort. It's nice to have the chance to dress up for a change,' she added, wishing she could hurt him as easily as he seemed to be able to hurt her. 'I don't get much opportunity at Bushman's Creek, do I?'

The edge in her voice was wasted on Gray. 'I guess not,' he said.

'You don't like it, do you?'

The grey eyes that met his were bright with challenge, and he sighed and thrust his hands deeper into the pockets of his pale moleskin trousers. 'It's not that,' he said after a moment. 'It's just that you look different.'

'It's only a dress,' said Clare. 'I'm exactly the same as I've always been.'

Gray looked at her, unsmiling. 'I know,' he said. He opened the door, as if bored by the subject. 'Alice is sleeping. Shall we go?'

She didn't care what he thought. What would Gray know about clothes, anyway? Clare put up her chin and walked past him. It felt good to be wearing nice clothes again, and that was what mattered, she decided, but as they waited for

the lift she found herself wishing that she had worn the simple pale pink shirt that he had unbuttoned so tantalisingly that afternoon instead.

The restaurant was obviously popular, and if Gray hadn't reserved a table they would never have been able to get in. It was humming with conversation and the sound of clinking glasses. Clare was very aware of Gray as they followed a waiter to their table. As usual, he was dressed with restraint, and did nothing to draw attention to himself, but there was something about his understated assurance, about his lean, powerful build and the easy way he moved, that drew the eye.

Clare felt ridiculously self-conscious as she sat opposite him, pretending to read the menu. Only that afternoon they had made love, with the sunshine pouring onto the bed, and now they were treating each other like strangers.

She couldn't look at him properly. Her eyes skittered between the menu and the glasses, between the cutlery and the other tables, and when they had ordered she sat desperately trying to think of something to say to break the tension twanging in the air. She fiddled with her fork, spinning it on the tablecloth, until Gray reached across the table and took it firmly away from her.

'What are you so nervous about?' he asked irritably.

'I don't know,' she confessed. 'I feel as if I'm on a first date. It's stupid, isn't it?'

Gray obviously thought that it was. 'Are you this jittery on all first dates?'

'I wasn't with Mark,' said Clare, remembering. 'It felt completely right together from the start.'

Gray's face closed. 'I don't expect you to feel the same with me, but there's still no need for you to be so jumpy. It's not as if we don't know each other!'

'I know. I think it's just seeing you out of context,' she

tried to explain. 'I'm used to you in the outback. It feels odd to be with you in a place like this.'

'I'm just the same here as I am anywhere else.'

'Perhaps it's me that's different, then.' Clare fingered the stem of her glass. 'I said I was the same in spite of the dress, but I don't think that's quite true. I feel different here. Walking around the streets tonight reminded me of home. I've got a great job. It can be hectic, and we spend most of our time teetering on the brink of a crisis, but there's something about working with creative people that gives me a real buzz. I need that adrenaline, I think.'

Gray had been watching her wistful expression as she remembered her life in London. 'No wonder you're bored in the outback,' he said, his voice flat and hard.

She looked up at that. 'I haven't been bored. You know what it's like looking after Alice. I never have time to be bored.'

'It's not what you're used to, though, is it?'

'No, but I'm getting used to it. I couldn't spend my whole life there,' she added with would-be carelessness, 'but I don't mind for a while. I think it's just that coming to a city has unsettled me.'

Gray waited until the waiter had poured the wine. 'Are you trying to tell me that you've changed your mind?' he asked with brutal directness when he had gone.

'Changed my mind?'

'About the wedding.'

'No!' Panic flitted across Clare's face and her fingers whitened around her glass. 'I mean...of course not. I have to get married so that I can stay in Australia!'

'We can get married here, if you'd rather,' said Gray, not looking at her. 'It would be riskier, if the immigration authorities check up on the marriage, but I'm sure we could make some arrangement for you to stay in Perth if that's

what you want. I've got friends here who would help you. You wouldn't need to go back to Bushman's Creek.'

Not go back to Bushman's Creek? Clare's eyes darkened with dismay. Never hear the corellas shrieking and squabbling by the creek? Never watch the sun set over the distant blue ranges? Never sit on the dark verandah with Gray?

And which Clare can't bear the thought of that? asked a mocking voice inside her. Clearly not the one she was trying so hard to prove she was.

She pushed the voice aside and moistened her lips. 'I think it would be better if we went ahead as we've planned,' she said, not quite steadily. 'Alice is settled at Bushman's Creek, and I'm happy to stay with her as long as I'm needed. I know it won't be for ever, and if the authorities *do* check up we want it to look like a real marriage as long as necessary.'

To her horror, Clare could hear a pleading note creeping into her voice, and she stopped, avoiding his eyes.

Gray looked at her narrowly as he refilled her glass. 'If you're sure...'

'I am,' she snapped. Did he want her to go down on bended knee and beg?

'In that case, I'm going to see my lawyer tomorrow afternoon. I'll get him to draw up a legal agreement before the wedding, as we decided, and you'll have a get-out clause whenever you want.'

'And your own get-out clause?'

'That will be included, of course,' said Gray evenly. 'We should buy a wedding ring tomorrow, too, and you'd better get yourself a dress.'

Clare regained her equilibrium as they discussed practicalities. Sensible, city Clare was on safe ground talking about invitations and catering arrangements. It was much easier to treat marriage as an artificial exercise when weigh-

ing up the merits of marquees and collapsible tables with Gray than when she had to think about how it would feel to marry him, and how it would feel to say goodbye.

Before they had left Bushman's Creek, Clare had drawn up a long list of things she and Alice would need for the next few months, and she was looking forward to stocking up on a few luxuries too, but somehow she didn't enjoy her shopping trip the next afternoon as much as she had expected.

Gray was busy with various business appointments, but before they went their separate ways, he took Clare to a jeweller's, where they chose a plain gold wedding band and a beautiful diamond ring. Clare protested that an engagement ring was unnecessary, but Gray insisted.

'You can leave them when you go if you don't like them,' he said indifferently.

The diamonds glinted on Clare's finger, distracting her all afternoon. The shops were stylish and welcoming, and the choice overwhelming after the general store in Mathison, but she couldn't concentrate. She felt lop-sided without Gray.

She tried telling herself that it was just because it would have been easier if he had been able to take Alice while she looked around, but deep down she knew that it was more than that. She missed his quiet presence and his easy stride. She missed his dry humour and the way he looked down at her sometimes with that smile lurking in his eyes. She missed being able to turn her head and know that he was there.

Really, it was ridiculous, thought Clare crossly as she let herself back into the hotel room. A whole afternoon in a wonderful city like Perth, and she had spent most of it missing a man who belonged out in that far, sunburnt country, with the silence and the shimmering heat and the wide, empty horizon.

'So much for being a city girl,' she sighed.

CHAPTER SEVEN

IT WAS impossible to settle. Clare sat on the bed with Alice and they examined their purchases together, but all the time she was listening for the sound of Gray at the door, and she jumped at the slightest noise. When at last he did come back, the sight of him in the doorway sent her heart leaping into her throat, where it lodged, beating wildly.

If only she could be like Alice, whose face lit up when she saw him and who could stretch out her arms, secure in the knowledge that he would pick her up with a smile and hug her against him! Clare could only smile stiffly, paralysed by an absurd shyness.

'Did you have a good time?' he asked, throwing Alice in the air so that she shrieked with excitement.

'Great,' she lied, horribly aware that her voice sounded high and unconvincing. She wanted to ask him if he had missed them, but she didn't dare. Instead she got up and moved away from the terrible temptation to hold out her arms like Alice and beg to be held and smiled at too. 'Shall I book the babysitting service again for this evening?' she asked, for something to say.

'No need.' Gray caught Alice for the final time and tucked her into his arm. 'We're having dinner with Lizzy tonight.' He tickled Alice's nose. 'She can't wait to meet *you*!'

'When was this arranged?' asked Clare, dangerously quiet.

'I rang her as soon as I knew when we'd be coming to

Perth, and then I called her this afternoon to confirm. This evening suits Lizzy best.'

'And what if it doesn't suit me?'

He lifted an eyebrow in surprise. 'You haven't made any other arrangements, have you?'

'That's not the point!' Clare was furious with herself. A whole afternoon she had wasted missing Gray, and all the time he had been thinking about tonight and seeing his precious Lizzy again! 'You could have asked me,' she pointed out, angry and humiliated.

'Look, what's the problem?' asked Gray, an edge of exasperation creeping into his voice. 'You're the one the misses the social life at Bushman's Creek, and now you've got an opportunity to go out and *be* social. You'll like Lizzy. She's a good friend of mine—and of Jack's—and we always see her when we're in Perth.'

'Why don't you go on your own, then?'

His mouth hardened. 'Because Lizzy's looking forward to meeting you and Alice. I told her about our engagement, and she would think it very strange if you don't go tonight. Besides, it's a special occasion. We're supposed to be having a double celebration. I haven't seen Lizzy since she announced *her* engagement, and she wants me to meet her fiancé.'

'Oh, I *see*,' said Clare bitterly. 'Lizzy's got a fiancé, so you need to prove that you've got one, too. No wonder you were so keen for me to have an engagement ring.' She thrust out her hand, scowling down at the glittering diamonds on her finger. 'I've got to have all the trappings or Lizzy might be suspicious. That's why you bought the ring, isn't it?' The grey eyes glittered as she glared at him. '*Isn't* it?'

'No.'

Clare was thrown by the bald reply. 'What do you mean, *no*?'

'No, that isn't the reason I bought you the ring,' said Gray evenly, although a muscle beating in his jaw indicated that he was only keeping hold of his temper with difficulty.

'They why did you buy it?' she challenged him.

He looked coldly back at her. 'Right now, Clare, I don't feel like telling you.'

Clare dressed to go out in a mood of simmering resentment. She knew that Gray thought she was being unreasonable, and it didn't make her feel any better to suspect that she thought so too. She didn't know why she felt so angry. It wasn't as if any of it was a surprise, and at least now she knew why they had come all the way to Perth, when Darwin was much closer to Bushman's Creek.

It was just the idea of him making plans to see her behind her back, Clare seethed. She knew how he felt about Lizzy, but still...he could have told her!

'What have you told Lizzy about us?' Clare broke the jangling silence in the car as they drove out to the suburb where Lizzy lived.

'I said you were working at Bushman's Creek and that we were engaged.'

'So Lizzy's not expecting me to confirm any romantic stories about how we fell in love at first sight or anything unlikely like that?'

'No.' Gray changed gear as they approached a red light. 'I just told her that I'd fallen in love with you.'

There was an airless pause. 'Didn't she want to know why?' Clare longed to sound amused at the very idea, but her voice sounded tight and strained instead.

'Of course she did,' he said with some acidity. 'Women always want to know why.'

'So what did you say?'

He glanced at her, then back to the road. 'I said she would understand when she saw you.'

Disconcerted, Clare felt her cheeks burn with sudden colour, and she turned her face away to stare fixedly out of the window. 'Does that mean you're going to tell Lizzy the truth?' she asked, unsure how to interpret his words. His face and voice were so empty of expression that it was impossible to tell whether he was being serious or sarcastic.

'I don't think we should tell anyone the truth,' said Gray. 'Not even Lizzy. Not yet.'

Not *even* Lizzy, Clare noted, and folded her lips. By the time they reached the house she was dreading the evening ahead, and prepared to dislike Gray's ex-fiancée intensely, but it was impossible not to like Lizzy. She was tall and striking, rather than beautiful, with a mass of blonde hair, a wide, humorous mouth and a vivid personality that reminded Clare achingly of Pippa.

She and Gray were obviously close. Clare tried not to notice how tightly he hugged Lizzy, or the unmistakable affection in his smile as he greeted her, and she wondered how Lizzy really felt about apparently losing him to Clare. Even if she was in love with someone else, she might well feel possessive about Gray's friendship, but she turned to Clare with unshadowed friendliness and there was no hint of jealousy in her manner.

'Gray said you were beautiful, and you are!' she exclaimed, and Clare couldn't forbear from a startled glance at Gray. Had he really said she was beautiful? 'I'm so thrilled about you two getting married,' Lizzy was chattering on, linking her arm with Clare's and sweeping her into the house on a tide of warmth. 'Gray's been waiting a long time for you!'

She introduced them proudly to her fiancé, Stephen. Clare watched him shake hands with Gray and thought that

the two men could hardly have been more different. Apart from the fact that they were both tall, and both in love with Lizzy, they appeared to have nothing in common.

Stephen was slighter than Gray, and darkly handsome, with an intense, artistic manner and an air of smouldering passion. To Clare he seemed vaguely familiar. It was a few minutes before she realised that he reminded her of Mark, and she was surprised to discover that instead of the expected pang she felt only satisfaction at solving something that had been puzzling her.

Lizzy and Gray were exchanging news of mutual friends—or, rather, Lizzy was bombarding Gray with gossip and he was listening with a lurking smile that made Clare turn abruptly to Stephen. She was delighted when he told her that he was a musician. It meant they could have a conversation nearly as animated as the one Gray and Lizzy were enjoying.

Stephen was good company. He had an engaging wit, and as they knew a number of people in common in the orchestral world he was very easy to talk to. It wasn't Stephen's fault that her attention kept being distracted by the easy intimacy between Gray and Lizzy, or that she noticed every time Gray smiled at Lizzy, or touched her with affection.

By the end of the evening Clare's jaw ached with the effort of keeping a smile fixed to her face. Lizzy was so vivacious that there had been no awkward silences, but even so, she was aware of a tension around the table. Gray had grown increasingly terse, and his manner to Stephen bordered on the hostile. He was obviously jealous, and just as obviously Stephen was aware of it. On several occasions Clare had had to hurriedly draw his attention away from Gray, who'd spent most of the evening sitting with a clenched jaw and his mouth set in a grim line.

It was a relief when he got up, interrupting Clare's conversation with Stephen about a famous conductor, and said that they would have to go. They collected Alice from the bedroom where she had been sleeping, and put her in the car.

'I'll see you at the wedding,' said Lizzy, giving Clare a warm hug. 'It's only a couple of weeks away, isn't it? You must be getting excited!'

'Oh, yes, very,' said Clare lamely, but fortunately Lizzy didn't seem to notice.

'I'm so glad I had a chance to meet you before I saw you coming down the aisle. You *are* getting married in Mathison church, I suppose?'

'No,' Gray answered for her. 'The wedding's going to be at Bushman's Creek.'

'You don't mean you're going to miss out on a traditional white wedding?' exclaimed Lizzy, obviously disappointed.

'We thought we'd keep the ceremony very simple,' said Clare. 'It's too far for any of my friends to come out, so a traditional wedding would be a bit lop-sided.'

'I hadn't thought of that,' said Lizzy contritely. 'But Stephen and I will be there,' she added, giving Clare another hug, 'and I hope you'll think of us as your friends!'

'She's lovely,' said Clare to Gray as they drove back through the dark streets.

'Yes,' he said, 'she is.'

A perverse instinct made her add, 'Stephen's nice, too.'

'You obviously thought so,' said Gray, with something of a snap.

Clare swung round in her seat. 'What do you mean by that?'

'You spent the whole evening flirting with him.'

'*Flirting…?*' gasped Clare, hardly able to believe her ears.

'Well, what else would you call the way you were carrying on, gazing into his eyes and talking about the music business all evening so that nobody else could join in?'

Clare was breathless at the unfairness of the accusation. 'I was not *carrying on,*' she said furiously. 'I was only talking to him because I felt sorry for him having to watch *you* mooning over Lizzy. It wasn't as if you made any effort to be pleasant. You ignored him all evening. It was perfectly obvious that you were jealous of him!'

'Jealous?' Gray snorted. 'Why would I be jealous of a man like that?'

'Because he's attractive, cultured, witty, intelligent…?' she suggested sweetly, and he cast her a glance of dislike.

'He's not man enough for Lizzy.'

'Why?' she asked tartly. 'Because he's interested in music and the arts rather than cows? You don't have to ride around looking macho on a horse and wrestle bulls to the ground to prove that you're a man, you know!'

Gray's hands tightened on the steering wheel. 'I'm well aware of what constitutes an ideal man as far as you're concerned! I'm just saying that Stephen doesn't have a strong enough personality to stand up to Lizzy.'

'Oh, rubbish!'

'What would you know about it?' he asked nastily. 'You hardly spoke to her all evening, you were so busy impressing Stephen with your famous contacts in the music world.'

'As it happens, I had a long chat with Lizzy in the kitchen before dinner, while you were making absolutely no effort to get on with Stephen,' said Clare coldly. 'She wanted to know all about us, so I had to make up a lot of totally implausible stories about how in love we were. Lizzy seemed to swallow them, though God knows why!'

she added, making no attempt to disguise her sarcasm. 'You weren't exactly giving the impression of an adoring fiancé. You hardly said a word to me all evening.'

'I didn't get a chance,' countered Gray. 'You were too busy finding Stephen witty and intelligent and attractive.'

'He *is* all those things, and Lizzy thinks so, too,' said Clare. 'She told me all about him and how they met. I know you don't want to hear it, but she's in love with him. I think they'll be very happy together.'

'Listen, all I want is for Lizzy to be happy. If I thought Stephen was the right man to make her happy I'd be the first to wish them well, but I don't think he will.'

'No, well, you wouldn't, would you?' Clare hunched her shoulders and glowered out of the window. 'If you had your way, Lizzy wouldn't be happy having a fantastic job in a wonderful city and being with a wonderful man; she'd be stuck up at Bushman's Creek instead and bored out of her mind!'

'The way you are?' said Gray in a hard voice.

'At least I only have to be there until your brother gets back!'

Dimly, Clare knew that she would regret what she had said, but she was tired and angry—with Gray for being so blind and pig-headed, with herself for caring *what* he was like. Close to tears, she turned her face away. It was one thing to know about Lizzy, quite another to meet her and like her and understand why Gray had loved her for so long.

The city lights blurred before her eyes. The streets in this part of town were still vibrant with life, and music and laughter spilled out onto the pavements. Wherever she looked there were people and buildings and noisy, cheerful activity. They crowded her vision, seeming to press claustrophobically around her, and she was seized by a sudden

longing, so acute that it was almost painful, to be back at Bushman's Creek, with the dust and the light and the glaring blue sky.

Tomorrow, she comforted herself. Tomorrow she would be back there. It would be quiet and still and they could go back to the way they had been before, before they'd come to the city and she'd got so muddled about what she really wanted.

They flew back the next afternoon. The moment Clare's feet touched the red outback earth again she felt steadier. It felt like coming home.

Everything that had seemed confused and unsettling in the city was somehow clearer in the crystalline light of Bushman's Creek. Clare looked back on those snappy exchanges with Gray and wondered why she had let herself get so upset. She had accused Gray of being jealous, but she had been behaving as if *she* was, she realised uncomfortably. It was none of her business how Gray felt about Lizzy, she reminded herself. They had an agreement and she should have stuck to it.

Instead, she had spoiled everything. The atmosphere, which had been so relaxed when they'd left Bushman's Creek was now constrained. Last night they had lain rigidly apart in the hotel bed, and now she didn't know whether Gray was expecting her to move back to the room she had shared with Alice or not.

Well, she couldn't spend the next few months feeling like this, Clare decided practically. Ignoring the strain between them would just make things worse.

When she had put Alice to bed that evening, she went to find Gray. He was leaning on the verandah rail, a bottle of beer in one hand, gazing out into the darkness with a preoccupied expression. At the sound of Clare's footsteps

he straightened, and, setting his beer down on the top of the rail, he turned to face her.

Clare stopped, and they looked wordlessly at each other for what seemed like a long time. By the time she moved forward to stand beside him, she felt that they had already had the most important part of their conversation. Still without speaking, they leant together on the rail. A huge yellow moon hung low in the sky and the night air reverberated with the sound of insects shrilling.

'I came to say that I was sorry,' said Clare at last.

'You don't need to be sorry for anything,' he said, and she could feel his eyes on her face.

'I think I do,' she told him quietly. 'I behaved badly in Perth. I don't know why I was so on edge.'

'Don't you?'

She sighed a little. 'Well, yes, I suppose I do. Being there reminded me too much of my life at home, and I felt...' she searched for the right word '...torn.' She glanced up at his austere profile. 'But I didn't mean some of the things I said to you last night. I was glad to come back here in the end, and I'm happy to stay as long as I'm needed.'

'You might be needed a very long time, Clare.' There was an odd note in Gray's voice, and she looked at him curiously for a moment before her eyes went back to the moon.

'I don't think so. When Jack comes back, he needs to become the most important person in Alice's life, and that would be easier if I wasn't around. I think it would be easier for me too,' she added honestly.

'So you'll go as soon as Jack returns?'

'If he accepts Alice as his daughter, yes, I think I should.'

Gray was silent for a while. 'I think I'm the one who needs to apologise,' he said eventually. 'I could have been a lot more understanding. Being in a city with you and

seeing how at home you were there made me realise how hard it must have been for you to adjust to life out here.'

'And I realised why Lizzy is so important to you,' said Clare, 'so we both learnt something.' She paused, smoothing the wooden rail beneath her hand, and then went on rather hesitantly, 'It's not an easy situation for either of us, but things were OK before we went to Perth, weren't they?'

He turned his head to look at her. 'Yes,' he said slowly, 'they were.'

'Do you think they could be like that again?' Clare asked.

'Making the most of a temporary relationship?' said Gray, as if he were quoting something he had learned by heart.

'Yes.' Clare swallowed. She didn't want to push him, but how else was she going to be able to cope with the next few months? 'We could…couldn't we?'

Slowly, Gray reached out and smoothed a strand of hair behind her ear. His smile was rather twisted as he let his hand slide to the nape of her neck to tug her, unresisting, towards him. 'We could try,' he said.

'Billy…tea…mugs…water…sandwiches,' Clare muttered to herself as she checked the contents of the box. 'Sugar!' she remembered, and spooned some into a jar before finding a place for it in the box next to a tin of biscuits and Alice's juice. 'OK, Alice, I think that's it,' she said, scooping the baby up from the floor and carrying her out to strap her into the car seat. 'We're ready to go!'

Ten days had passed since they had come back from Perth, and the morning before Gray had taken the men up to the top end of the station for a last big muster before the wedding. In spite of her brave words assuring Gray that she and Alice would be fine on their own, Clare hadn't

been looking forward to spending a whole day and night alone in the homestead, but in the end they really *had* been fine.

She hadn't been nearly as lonely as she had expected, at least not during the day. How could she feel alone with Alice, and when outside there were the dogs, the chickens, who tumbled over themselves in their haste to find out what scraps she had brought, and the horses who had been left behind to graze in the paddock? When from the bedroom window she could see big red kangaroos and the smaller, greyer wallabies with their gentle faces, who would sit up and stare at her with big eyes and twitching noses before lolloping off into the bush, and when down by the water-hole the trees were full of birds? They twittered, whistled, warbled, shrieked and squawked, until the cacophony died away at dusk leaving only the mournful kaarrk-kaarrk of the rooks.

No, Clare hadn't been lonely during the day, but it had been a very long night without Gray. The bed had felt empty and unwelcoming without him, and she had tossed and turned until the small hours. Now, as she loaded up the car, she tried to suppress a treacherous sense of excitement at the thought of seeing him again after a mere twenty-four hours. He had contacted her on the radio the evening before, and they had agreed that she would take lunch and meet them at one of the watering points before they brought the cattle in the last few thirsty miles.

They found the watering point without difficulty, bumping slowly across the paddock to park in the shade of a coolibah tree. Alice was burbling to herself in the back, and Clare folded her arms on the steering wheel and thought about the last ten days as they waited for the cattle to appear.

As soon as Gray had kissed her that night on the veran-

dah, she had known that everything would be all right. They had fallen easily back into their old routine, and after a while it had been hard to remember that there had ever been any constraint between them. It would have been impossible, in any case, to remain stiff for long when Alice was around. She was just starting to crawl, and was turning into a real clown, having already learnt that making them laugh was an excellent way to get their attention. She loved to be thrown in the air, or to jump up and down on their knees, jabbering with pleasure, and in her quieter moments she liked to play peekaboo between them in Gray's bed or to have kisses blown against her tummy.

Everything was working out very well, Clare thought, her eyes on a wallaby that had paused, suddenly alert, on the edge of the scrub. Alice was happy, Gray was happy, and she was happy, too. After Perth, the air had cleared, and it was somehow easier to treat the situation in a light-hearted way. It was no big deal, she told herself. She and Gray were enjoying themselves. Neither of them were involved. It was just fun, and if sometimes a shadow passed over her mind at the thought of saying goodbye, Clare wouldn't let herself dwell on it. Things were fine, and that was enough for now.

It wasn't long before the herd lumbered into sight through the boab trees and the towering termite mounds. The first few cows passed the car incuriously, but suddenly the landscape was swirling with red dust and the air was full of the sound of hooves and lowing cattle and the encouraging 'yips' of the stockmen. Clare caught glimpses of them through the confusion, effortlessly controlling the herd on their wild-looking horses.

One by one the men made their way towards her, and without their chivvying the cattle blundered to a halt, as if unsure what to do with themselves. After a while they low-

ered their heads to graze on the sparse tufts of dry brown grass, drifting gradually away from the humans and their horses.

The watering point was obviously a traditional stopping place. An area well away from the trees had been cleared for a fire, and the logs set around as seating were worn and polished with use. In no time at all Joe had kindled a fire and set the billy to boil for tea.

The other men sat around on the logs, rolling cigarettes or helping to keep Alice amused while Clare unloaded the lunch from the car. Alice was a favourite with them all, and they lost their shyness as they dandled her on their knees or made funny faces to make her laugh. Clare always found it touching to see how gentle they were with her, and how carefully they passed her from one to another with their big, callused hands.

'Where's Gray?' she asked, unwrapping sandwiches.

'He'll be along in a minute,' they told her. 'He was at the back, bringing in the stragglers.'

'There he is now,' said someone.

Clare turned, and without warning the earth dropped away from beneath her feet. Gray was riding towards her, and as she watched he pulled up his horse, swung easily out of the saddle, and tied it up with the others who stood patiently in the shade, twitching their tails and shaking their heads against the flies.

He took off his hat as he came towards them with that rangy, deliberate stride, wiping his forehead with the back of his arm, and Clare's heart turned over with the sudden, terrible realisation of how much she loved him.

Still clutching the sandwiches, Clare stood as if rooted to the spot. She felt hollow, faintly sick, as if she had just stepped over the edge of an abyss and was tumbling helplessly in a void. Why now? she wondered with an odd,

detached part of her mind. Why fall in love with him when he was hot and dusty and tired, and love was clearly the last thing on his mind?

Except that she hadn't just fallen in love with him, had she? With sudden clarity, Clare understood that she had been sliding inexorably into love with him ever since he had walked up the hotel steps and smiled at Alice. She just hadn't wanted to accept it until now.

'Clare? Are you all right?' Gray was looking at her narrowly, and she started, colour surging up her cheeks as she realised that she was just standing there, staring at him, and that the other men were regarding her curiously.

'I'm fine,' she said, appalled to hear her words come out as no more than a croak. Clearing her throat, she tried again. 'Sorry, I was…dreaming.'

Her knees were shaking and, afraid that they would simply give way altogether, she sat down abruptly on one of the logs.

'Sure?' Gray persisted. 'You look very odd.'

'I'm just hot,' said Clare, with an edge of desperation, and thrust the sandwiches at Ben in an effort to change the subject. 'Here, have some lunch.'

The men wolfed down the sandwiches and the biscuits, but she couldn't eat anything. She took some tea when Joe handed her a black brew in a battered enamel mug and held it between her hands, staring down into it as she struggled to absorb the enormity of her discovery.

Why, why, why had she had to fall in love with him? She had had enough of hopeless love, Clare thought in desperation. She didn't want to love Gray. She wanted to go on thinking that everything was fine, that a light-hearted affair was enough and that when the time came she would be able to say goodbye.

Only it was too late for that now.

She had loved Mark, but not like this. Intense, turbulent, exciting—even at the time her love for Mark had had a dream-like quality. It had offered an escape from a humdrum routine, and with her new clarity Clare wondered how long it would have lasted faced with the day-to-day practicalities of life.

Loving Gray was something quite different. This time, love hadn't swept her off her feet as it had with Mark. It had crept up on her, coiling its tendrils around her and binding her fast before she knew what was happening to her. And then she had turned and seen Gray walking towards her, and had recognised him for what he was: her anchor, her security, the fixed point in her life around which everything else revolved. Gray, the man whose mere presence could steady a reeling and uncertain world, the man who could set her senses singing with the brush of his fingers.

Nothing would ever be the same again. She would never be able to pretend now that she was just 'making the best of things'. Why couldn't she have carried on believing that what she felt for him was no more than physical attraction? It had been so much easier then. It was as if a huge gulf had opened up between the person she was now, knowing that she loved him, and the woman she had been before she had turned to see him swing off his horse and walk towards her.

When she remembered how she had assured Gray that she wouldn't get involved, Clare didn't know whether to laugh or cry at her own blindness. It was so obvious. It had always been obvious! Only a fool could have resisted the truth for so long.

Clare drank her tea, her heart awash with a mixture of exultation and despair. Part of her longed to shout her love out loud, another dreaded Gray's reaction if she did. She

could imagine his face closing in appalled disbelief. It would put an intolerable pressure on him to make more of the marriage than he wanted, and that wouldn't be fair.

You don't need to worry, she had promised him. *I won't get emotionally involved. I'm not taking it seriously.*

How wrong she had been!

Around her, Clare was vaguely conscious of the slow drawls discussing the muster, but the other men and the vast expanse of the outback behind them seemed to exist in a blur. Only Gray was real, immediate, *there*. He sat next to her on the log, a mug of tea in one hand, Alice held on his knee with the other. He had given her a crust of bread and she was sucking it happily, evidently feeling quite safe and secure in his firm grasp.

Overwhelmed by a ridiculous shyness, Clare stared fixedly down at her tea, but she was still excruciatingly aware of him beside her, and her eyes kept crawling back to him. It was as if he were outlined in preternatural detail against the sky, and she could see every crease at the edges of his eyes, every one of the fine hairs at his wrist, every line in his hand. He was unshaven after a night under the stars, and Clare's fingers prickled as if she had brushed them against the stubble on his jaw.

There was a fine layer of dust on his skin and a pulse beating steadily, irresistibly, in his throat. It beckoned her, almost taunting. He was so close, and it would be so easy to lean towards him and touch her lips to it, to kiss her way up over his rough, dusty jaw to the dent at the corner of his mouth. The urge to do just that was so strong that Clare moved jerkily further down the log, terrified that she would be unable to stop herself from twining round him.

Dizzy with desire, she wanted to dash the mug from his hand. Stop talking about horses! she wanted to shout. Stop thinking about how many cattle got away or whether the

road train will have any difficulty getting over the range! Tell them all to go away and take me in your arms. Lay me down in the red dust and tell me you'll never let me go.

She could imagine it so clearly that when Gray put down his mug in the dirt and turned to her Clare's every sense leapt in sudden fear that she had spoken aloud. But he didn't reach for her. He simply said that they should move on before the cattle wandered too far, and stood up.

He carried Alice over to the car while Clare gathered up what was left of lunch with shaking hands and Ben doused the fire and stamped out the embers. By the time she had put everything away, the stockmen were all back on their horses and heading off, and Gray had settled Alice into her car seat.

He waited until Clare had closed the back of the car. 'Are you sure you're all right, Clare?' he asked, frowning. 'You've been very quiet.'

Her eyes slid away from his. 'Yes, really.' Lifting her left hand, she pushed her hair behind her ear in an unconsciously nervous gesture, and the diamonds on her finger flashed in the sun. 'I'm fine.' She managed a smile. 'I expect it's just pre-wedding nerves.'

Gray nodded as if he understood. 'Only four more days. It'll be over soon.'

He meant the wedding, but his words were like a knife turning in Clare's heart. Tears stung her eyes and she turned quickly away to get into the car. Everything would be over soon. Jack would come back, and she would have to say goodbye and spend the rest of her life trying to forget Gray. 'I know,' she said.

reed come with here any children getting over the missel' Tell them all to go away and be done in your rooms. Lay me down in the red. How me tell me world never let me go.

She said there? dimmer sat. It? sat, so now put down ring in the air and turned to there live a swan severe

CHAPTER EIGHT

CLARE turned in front of the mirror, lifting her arms so that the long gossamer jacket billowed gently around her like the wings of a moth. Beneath it, her dress was the palest of greys, the same silvery colour as her eyes, and the silk felt cool and luxurious against her skin. It's my wedding day, she kept saying to herself, but it seemed impossible to take in.

'It's my wedding day,' she told her reflection out loud, and practised a smile that didn't really go with the wistful expression in her eyes. 'In a few minutes I'm going to walk out of that door and marry the man that I love. So why do I look so sad?'

She knew why, of course. She loved Gray, but she didn't want to be marrying him like this. She didn't want to be second best. She wanted Gray to marry her because he loved her and not because he couldn't have Lizzy. And she wanted to marry *him* knowing that they loved and needed each other, and could spend the rest of their lives together.

Her fingers crept to the fine strand of pearls at her throat. The necklace had been Pippa's, inherited from their mother, and she had given it to Clare to keep in trust for Alice. Today of all days Clare wanted to wear it and remember her sister, and she touched the pearls like a talisman, to remind her of what this marriage really meant. She was marrying Gray for Alice, and for Pippa.

Saddened by her own reflection, Clare turned away and picked up the photograph of her sister which she kept in a frame by the bed. Pippa's vivid, pretty face laughed back

at her, and Clare's throat tightened unbearably as grief clawed at her heart. She had thought she was getting used to losing Pippa, but there were times, like now, when she missed her sister's warmth and laughter with a physical ache.

This should have been Pippa's day. She should have been the bride, marrying the man she loved under the ghost gums, and Gray should have been an onlooker instead of the groom, going through the motions with the wrong woman.

But it wasn't Pippa's wedding day; it was hers. Clare touched the photograph lovingly and set the frame down just as Gray came into the bedroom after a brief knock on the door. He was formally dressed in a dinner jacket and bow tie, and the severe lines and dazzling white of his shirt made him look somehow formidable, browner and tougher and unfamiliar.

'Are you ready?'

'Almost.' Clare turned her face away, but not before he had seen that her eyes were huge and shimmering with tears.

Reaching behind him, Gray closed the door and looked across the room at the woman who was about to become his wife. The luminous grey of her dress almost exactly matched the colour of her eyes, and the silk glistened through the sheer material of the jacket as she stood there, dark and slender and sad, with a single flower in her hair.

'Clare?' he said quietly.

Clare didn't—couldn't—answer. Rigid with the effort of not crying, she kept her back to him and covered her trembling mouth with her hand.

Without another word, Gray crossed the room and wrapped his arms around her, pulling her against him so

that he could rest his cheek against her shining dark hair. 'Don't cry, Clare,' he said.

Clare resisted at first, but after a moment she abandoned her pride and let herself lean against his hard, reassuring body while she struggled to do as he asked and swallow the sudden, scalding tears.

'I know this isn't the wedding you wanted,' Gray went on, his deep voice vibrating through her, 'but it will be all right, I promise you. Getting married seems like a big step, but I won't hold you to anything; you know that. You can go whenever you want. It's not going to be for ever.'

'I know,' whispered Clare. That was what hurt so much.

She let him comfort her instead with the hard strength of his body. Leaning against him felt like coming home, and she clung to him, hiding her face in his throat so that she could breathe in the familiar scent of his skin. She could feel his heart beating, slow and steady, the warmth of his hand through the slippery silk, and slowly she absorbed his massive calm.

'It's not going to be for ever,' Gray had said, but he might change his mind. Lizzy was getting married, and once he had accepted that she was never coming back he might be ready to start again. Clare would be there; he might come to love her. It wasn't impossible, was it? If Jack stayed away long enough, maybe Gray would get used to being married to her. Maybe, when Jack returned, he would ask her to stay. Maybe this time loving wouldn't be so hopeless.

Drawing a long, steadying breath, she made herself step away from him. 'I'm OK now. Thanks.'

'Are you sure?' Still holding her by the hands, Gray looked at her with concern.

She nodded, and made a brave attempt at a smile which didn't quite come off. 'Thanks. I was just being silly.'

'It's not too late to change your mind, you know,' he said, as if the words were forced out of him.

'I don't want to change my mind.' Clare's voice was steadier now and she took another breath as she looked straight at him. 'I want to marry you.'

The brown eyes held a strange expression as he looked back at her, and his hold on her hands tightened for a moment before he let her go.

'Then, shall we go and get married?' he said.

Clare managed a better smile this time. 'Yes, let's do that.' Picking up the simple spray of flowers, she walked with him along the corridor and out onto the verandah. At the top of the steps, Gray paused and held out his hand, and she put hers into it without hesitation, her heart clenching as his fingers closed securely around it.

Hand in hand, they walked out to the creek. It was five o'clock, Clare's favourite time, when the glare of the day faded and the distant ranges blurred into a purplish blue. A strange silence fell over the land and the air was filled with a hush of anticipation before dusk. Even the birds in the trees overhanging the waterhole were quiet.

Although people had been arriving since the day before, and the airstrip was lined with single-engined planes, Clare was still surprised at how many people seemed to be waiting for them. She had an impression of a mass of smiling faces, and then Lizzy, holding Alice in the pretty smocked dress and matching hat that Clare had bought in Perth.

After that, Clare didn't remember very much. They had agreed on a simple ceremony, and she supposed they must have made their vows before the celebrant, although later all she could remember was the warm, firm clasp of Gray's hand, and the moment when he slid the ring onto her finger. She remembered, too, the expression in his deep brown eyes, how he had smiled as he bent his head, and the way

their lips had caught and clung in a kiss so sweet that she'd ached when he let her go.

And then it was over. There were cheers and whistles, and suddenly Clare found herself being kissed and congratulated. A few of the faces she recognised from Mathison, but most people were strangers to her, and she was soon dizzy with introductions. It was a relief to see Lizzy at her side, with Alice in her arms.

As soon as she saw Clare, Alice's face broke into an irresistible smile and she stretched out her arms. Clare took her, cuddling her warm, solid, sweet-smelling weight against her, and kissing the downy hair on top of her head.

'So, how does it feel to be a married woman?' asked Lizzy, smiling.

Clare's eyes rested on Gray. She saw him smile as he had his hand wrung by Joe, and she was gripped by a sudden rush of happiness. This might not be marriage quite the way she wanted it, but at least she was with the man she loved, and tonight, when the party was over, he would close the bedroom door on everyone else and they would be alone. For now, thought Clare, it was enough.

She smiled at Lizzy. 'It feels good,' she said.

'Stephen's so sorry he couldn't make it,' said Lizzy. 'He's had to go to Sydney to play in some concert. He sent you his love, though.'

'I'm sorry he's not here, too,' said Clare. She glanced hesitantly at Lizzy. Although the other girl was smiling, she sensed an underlying trouble, and she hoped that Lizzy and Stephen weren't having problems.

She had wanted Stephen there, not just because she liked him, but because she'd wanted Gray to see that Lizzy was firmly attached to another man. Now Lizzy was here on her own, and Clare wondered whether Gray would look at her and let himself think of what might have been.

But there was no trace of regret in Gray's manner when he came over a moment later and kissed Lizzy's cheek, and after a while Clare made herself stop worrying about it. This was her wedding day, after all, and she might as well enjoy it.

Champagne was circulating, and in no time at all, it seemed, the party was in full swing. Clare stayed close to Gray, reassured by the feel of his fingers laced with hers, or his hand at her waist as he introduced her to his friends and relatives. Everyone asked after Jack, and said what a pity it was he couldn't be at the wedding.

'We haven't been able to contact him,' explained Gray for the umpteenth time. 'He's gone walkabout in South America.'

'Couldn't you have waited until he got back?' asked one of his aunts, a gaunt woman with shrewd eyes and a smile, Clare discovered, of unexpected charm.

'We don't know when he'll come home. It might not be for months.' Gray put his arm around Clare. 'And I've waited long enough for the right woman. I didn't feel like waiting any longer.'

He was acting the part so well, thought Clare with a tiny pang. She would have to be careful. If she let herself, she could so easily believe that he meant it.

His aunt shook her head, amused. 'You haven't changed,' she said. 'He was just the same when he was a little boy,' she told Clare. 'Stubborn as anything! He'd wait patiently until he'd decided exactly what he wanted, but once he had nothing and nobody was going to stop him until he'd got it!'

Clare smiled at Gray, liking the idea of him as a little boy. 'Pig-headed, I see!'

'I just know what I want,' he said evenly, 'and now I've got it.'

Silver-grey eyes looked into brown, and for a moment it was as if the two of them were quite alone in the world, cut off from the talk and the laughter around them by a bubble of silence. There was a constriction in Clare's chest, making it hard for her to breathe. Gray was acting...wasn't he?

Vaguely, she was aware that someone was asking whether they were planning a honeymoon. 'Not at the moment,' said Gray, tearing his eyes from Clare's. 'It's a busy time on the station, and with Jack away I can't take more than a couple of days off. We'll be clearing up tomorrow, and then it will be back to work as usual on Monday.'

'That's not much fun for you, Clare.'

'I don't mind.' Clare's voice sounded husky to her own ears and she cleared her throat. It was time she played her part too. 'I knew what was involved when I said I'd marry you, didn't I?' she said, and Gray's brown eyes flickered.

'We both did,' he acknowledged.

'Never mind, you can have a proper honeymoon when Jack comes back,' said Gray's aunt, oblivious to the unspoken message passing between them. 'He can run the station and you two will be free to do whatever you want.'

They would indeed, thought Clare sadly, but not in the way his aunt meant. Everything would change when Jack came back. She wasn't going to think of what would happen then, though, she reminded herself. Not today, anyway. It was her wedding day, and she could ignore the future if she wanted to. Now was all that mattered.

So she smiled and leant against Gray, as if she were an ordinary bride confident that a lifetime of love and happiness lay ahead of her. 'I don't mind what we do, as long as we can do it together,' she said, and as Gray's arm tightened around her she hoped that he didn't know that she was speaking only the truth.

Bushman's Creek had been transformed for the wedding. A large open-sided marquee had been erected near the creek, and the tables were decorated with exquisite arrangement of native flowers, while Clare's kitchen had been taken over by an army of caterers flown in especially from Darwin. Clare, who had wondered how on earth she was going to cope with feeding such a large number, was left with nothing to do but let herself be swept along by the warmth and welcome of the outback community.

After the buffet, the tables were cleared from the middle of the marquee and there was dancing to a band. The most suspicious of immigration officers would never suspect that this was anything but an ordinary, joyous wedding, thought Clare as she danced with Gray later that night. Certainly none of the guests had guessed that things were not as they seemed.

They all seemed to be having a wonderful time, spilling out of the marquee to talk and laugh under the stars, almost everyone having moved on from champagne to beers that were being served in the cookhouse. Glancing around her, Clare couldn't see that anybody was in the slightest bit worried about how they were to get home.

'They'll go home tomorrow,' said Gray when she told him.

'But where are they all going to sleep?' she asked in surprise, and he smiled that smile that always made her shiver inside.

'They're not planning on sleeping! There aren't a lot of opportunities for socialising out here, so when one comes along, we all make the most of it!'

'I'm glad they're all having a good time.' Clare hesitated, then glanced up at Gray. 'Thank you for making it such a convincing wedding. It must have cost you an awful lot of money.'

'You don't need to thank me,' he said, and the harshness in his voice took her by surprise. 'Everyone has been waiting so long for me to get married that the least I can do for them is to lay on a good party. If we'd kept it a quiet affair they really *would* have been suspicious.'

"Do you think anyone suspects that we are not...you know...?"

'In love?' Gray lifted an eyebrow. 'Why would they?'

'Oh, I don't know...' Clare was beginning to wish they had not started this conversation. It was getting a little too close for comfort. 'I suppose I always thought it was obvious if a couple weren't really in love.'

'Perhaps we're good actors,' he suggested ironically.

He was, anyway. 'Perhaps,' she agreed, her eyes sliding away from his.

There was a pause. The music was slow and sensuous, and Clare was very aware of Gray's arms around her, of the hardness of his body, of the nearness of his skin. If she turned her head, she would be able to press her lips to his throat.

An ordinary bride would be able to kiss her husband without thinking. She would be able to whisper 'I love you' without being afraid that she would betray herself.

But she wasn't an ordinary bride, and if she wanted Gray to love her she would have to be very careful not to make him feel that he was being pushed into something he didn't want.

'I...I think I'd better go and check on Alice,' she muttered instead.

'I'll come with you,' said Gray, letting her go.

'There's no need—' Clare began, but he didn't let her finish.

'What's everyone going to think if I let my wife go wandering off on her own on our wedding night?'

Taking her hand, he led her out of the marquee and back towards the homestead along the creek. The sky was like spangled velvet, so crowded with stars that they seemed a blurry mass above the trees. Clare's sheer jacket floated insubstantially with every movement and the silvery sheen of her dress shimmered in the starlight as they walked through the shadows between the palely glimmering trunks of the ghost gums.

She was intensely aware of her surroundings, of the rasping whirr of the insects in the trees and the drifting scent of eucalyptus as they crushed the dry leaves beneath their feet. The smoothness of the silk slipping sensuously against her skin filled her with a drumming sense of anticipation. She had never been so conscious of her own body before, or of Gray's. He walked beside her in silence, his face obscured by the shadows, but the feel of his hand sharp and clear in every detail. Clare was sure that she could feel every callus on his palm, every whorl on his fingertips.

Alice was asleep. Exhausted by all the unfamiliar faces and activity, she hadn't stirred since Clare had slipped away from the party earlier to put her to bed. Lizzy had offered to look after Alice for her, but Clare had wanted to spend some time alone with Pippa's daughter on this day of all days. If it hadn't been for Alice she would never have come to Bushman's Creek. She would never have met Gray, never have fallen in love with him, never have married him.

Leaning over the cot, Clare adjusted the covering over the sleeping baby with a tender expression. As she straightened, the new ring on her finger gleamed dully in the reflected light through the window, and she looked down at it as if she had never seen it before. She was *married*. She turned the ring on her finger. It hadn't seemed real until

now, standing in the dark room with the tall, quiet man who was now her husband.

Slowly, Clare lifted her eyes to find Gray watching her. 'What is it?' he asked.

'We're married,' she said in a peculiar voice, as if it had only just struck her.

'We are,' Gray agreed. Walking round the cot, he took Clare's hands in his. 'You looked beautiful today, Clare,' he said, very deep and low. 'I was proud of you.'

'Really?'

He nodded. 'I watched you,' he said, his clasp warm and sustaining. 'You talked to everyone and you smiled and you made them all think that you were a bride like any other bride, and none of them guessed how hard it was for you.'

'No more than for you,' said Clare with difficulty.

Gray drew her closer. 'It wasn't hard for me,' he said.

'It wasn't really that hard for me either,' she told him. 'I just pretended it was real.'

'And did that help?'

'Yes,' she said slowly, twining her fingers around his. 'It helped a lot.'

Gray rubbed his thumb over the wedding ring. 'If it helps, perhaps we should just carry on pretending for a while?' he suggested, with a lurking smile that melted her bones.

'Perhaps we should,' smiled Clare, and they kissed softly in the darkness above the sleeping baby.

'Come on.' Gray led her across the corridor to his bedroom.

'What about everyone else?' she remembered reluctantly as he pulled her into the room and closed the door. 'Won't they wonder where we are?'

A smile flickered over his face. 'They're all having too

good a time to notice that we've gone, and if they did, I expect they could work out exactly where we are! It would look very odd if we stayed up partying all night when everyone would expect me to take the first opportunity to have my bride to myself.'

'True,' said Clare, pretending to consider the matter. 'And, since we want to be convincing,' she added, 'we might as well stay here and make the most of it, mightn't we?'

'Exactly,' said Gray, with a smile that made her heart pound. 'So come here, Mrs Henderson!'

Clare went.

Drumming with desire, she stood perfectly still as Gray peeled the gauzy jacket from her shoulders and let it drift to the floor like a cobweb. He lifted her hand and pressed a warm kiss to her palm before kissing the inside of her wrist and letting his lips travel deliciously up her arm, lingering in the tender inner elbow and on the curve of her shoulder and pulling her inexorably closer with every kiss until Clare felt as if she were unravelling with desire.

Unable to stay still any longer, she tugged at his shirt, pulling it free from his trousers, so that by the time he had kissed his way along her collarbone and up the side of her throat to her mouth she could run her hands over his back as they kissed hungrily.

Gray's fingers were warm against her spine as he slid the zip slowly downwards and eased the dress over her hips until it slithered off her in a whisper of silk. Clare shuddered with pleasure at the feel of his lips and his hands moving over her bare skin, and she arched against him, gasping his name, until Gray smiled into her throat.

'I think it's time I took my wife to bed,' he murmured.

* * *

It was light when she woke the next morning. Must be Sunday, she thought sleepily. On every other day of the week she was up before dawn to cook the men's breakfast.

Stirring languorously, Clare opened her eyes. There was sunshine slanting through the blinds and she was filled with a sense of well-being. She lay there blinking drowsily and wondering why she felt so contented, until the events of the day before filtered back into her mind.

They were married. She was Gray's wife. Lifting her hand, Clare studied the ring on her finger as if to convince herself that it was true, and her lips curved in a reminiscent smile as she remembered how the day had ended.

Clare stretched in the sunlight, her body still a-tingle as she remembered how Gray had made love to her. Last night, the passion between them had soared unstoppably to new heights, and afterwards they had laid entwined, rapt and wondering at what they had discovered together, murmuring breathless endearments as they drifted slowly back to earth. They might have been pretending, but it had felt oh! so real...

Gray couldn't make love to her like that and not feel *anything*, Clare convinced herself. It must be obvious how she felt, and if he wasn't yet ready to love her in the same way, then surely that would come. Filled with hope, if not certainty, she had been smiling when she fell asleep in his arms at last.

Still smiling with optimism, Clare rolled over to Gray, but the other side of the bed was empty. Disappointed not to find him there, she smoothed her hand over the sheet where he had lain. It would have been nice if he had been there, she thought with a tiny sigh, if his brown eyes had been smiling as he reached for her, if he had kissed her properly awake and reassured her that the night before had been more than just a dream.

She couldn't have everything, Clare tried to tell herself

sensibly. So it would have been perfect if they had been able to make love again slowly in the morning sunlight? It would have been perfect if he had told her that he loved her, too, but he didn't—or, at least, not yet—and in the meantime she could hope. There was no point in asking for more than he could give. She should be happy with what she had.

Remembering the night before, Clare thought that it would be enough—for now.

Outside, she could hear the birds in full voice down by the creek, but all was quiet in the homestead. Presumably everyone except Gray was sleeping off the effects of the night before. Clare reached over to the clock on Gray's side of bed. Alice was normally awake by now. She had better go and see if she was still asleep.

Pulling on a loose cotton robe, she bent to pick up the clothes that lay where they had left them last night. The dress was a silvery puddle on the floor, the gossamer jacket abandoned beside it. Clare smiled as she remembered how she had felt as Gray had peeled it from her shoulders, and hung it with the dress on a hanger. It would be hell to iron, but she didn't regret a single one of its creases.

She hung Gray's jacket on a hanger, too, folded his trousers over a chair and threw shirt and socks into the laundry basket before padding barefoot across the corridor to Alice's room.

The cot was empty. Gray must be giving her breakfast, thought Clare, and she made her way down to the kitchen, her feet making no sound on the smooth concrete floor. As she got closer, she could hear Alice gurgling to herself and banging her spoon on the highchair tray, and she smiled as she imagined Gray doggedly trying to get some food into her without most of it ending up on the floor or in her hair. The knack of feeding a baby continued to elude him.

Clare was still smiling as she reached the kitchen door. Alice spotted her first. 'Gah!' she cried, and held out her spoon, but Clare wasn't looking at her. She was staring over the highchair, her smile fading from her face. Gray was there, but he wasn't feeding Alice and he wasn't alone.

He was holding someone close, their heads bent tenderly together, and Clare knew instantly who it was.

It was Lizzy.

A cold hand gripped Clare's heart. She had known how Gray felt about Lizzy, but deep down she hadn't believed it until now, when she saw how intimately he held her, how right the two of them looked together.

Clare felt sick. She wanted to turn and run, to close her eyes to the sight of Lizzy in Gray's arms, to pretend that she had never seen them together, but she couldn't move. She could only stand and stare while all the hope and happiness she had woken with drained away.

'Gah!' said Alice again, more forcefully this time, and when she still didn't receive her due share of attention she threw her spoon on the floor.

The clatter made Gray lift his head, to see Clare staring across the room with a stricken expression.

'Clare!' he said, releasing Lizzy and making as if to step towards her.

Terrified that, given the slightest encouragement, she would burst into tears and betray herself completely, Clare chose the safest option and retreated behind a façade of chilly indifference. 'Don't mind me,' she said coldly as she moved forward to pick up Alice's spoon.

'I thought you were asleep,' said Gray.

That much was obvious, thought Clare bitterly. 'Really?'

His eyes narrowed at her tone. 'Alice and I came along to make you a cup of tea,' he persevered.

'And found me, crying all over your kitchen!' Lizzy put

in. She wiped her face and smiled waveringly at Clare, who realised for the first time that she had been crying. 'I'm sorry, Clare, I know this is a special morning for you. I didn't want to spoil it.'

She was clearly upset, but she didn't seem guilty, as she surely would have done if Clare had found her in a passionate embrace with Gray the day after their wedding. The savage claws of jealousy eased a little around Clare's heart.

'What's the matter?' she asked.

Lizzy drew a deep breath. 'I've decided not to marry Stephen,' she said.

'But…*why*?' Clare stared at her, appalled. Lizzy *had* to marry Stephen! How else could Gray let her go at last?

'I don't think we love each other enough,' said Lizzy sadly.

At least she hadn't said that she had realised that she was in love with Gray after all, thought Clare, clutching at straws. The fear that had gripped her when she had walked in to see Gray holding Lizzy, that they had decided they belonged together after all, had been the worst, but this was nearly as bad. Gray would never love her completely as long as Lizzy was free, as long as there was even a remote possibility that she could be his.

'You *do* love Stephen,' she said urgently. 'He's wonderful! He's intelligent and funny and talented and he loves you.' She saw Gray's face harden. He obviously didn't like her attempts to persuade Lizzy to stay with Stephen, but she pressed on anyway.

'Don't do anything rash, Lizzy. Stephen's a good man, and he's right for you. You'd miss him more than you know.'

'It's all right for you,' sniffed Lizzy. 'You've got Gray.'

'Believe me, I know what I'm talking about,' said Clare, not looking at Gray. 'The chance for real love doesn't come

along very often, and when it does you have to work to keep it.' That, after all, was what she was doing now. 'Don't throw away something that could be so special. You'll regret it for the rest of your life.'

'But that's the whole point!' said Lizzy tearfully. 'I'm not sure that what Stephen and I have *is* special. I watched the two of you together yesterday, and when you looked at each other it was as if there was nobody else in the world, and I realised that if I married Stephen, it wouldn't be like that. We don't have what you and Gray have.'

'It's…different…for us, Lizzy,' said Gray, with a warning glance at Clare.

'I know.' She nodded. 'That's what I mean. There's something about you both that lights up when the other's in the same room. You don't even have to be touching,' she told them wistfully. 'It's a kind of electricity in the air between you. That doesn't happen between Stephen and me.'

There was an uncomfortable little silence.

'But you and Stephen seemed so happy together,' said Clare rather desperately.

Lizzy sighed. 'Oh, yes, we get on well, and of course I'm very fond of him, but there isn't really a spark between us the way there is between you two. When I look back, I think we only got engaged because everyone else seemed to be getting married. We had lots in common and we were comfortable together, and we thought that would be enough, but now I've seen what a relationship should be like, I know it isn't. If I'm going to get married, I want it to be perfect.'

'Lizzy…' Clare looked at her helplessly. 'Lizzy, it's never perfect. You can't look at us. Every couple has their own reasons for getting married,' she went on, picking her words with care. 'Gray and I know what ours are, but they

wouldn't be the right reasons for you. Would they?' she added, with a defiant glance at Gray, but he didn't answer.

Lizzy ran her fingers wearily through her hair. 'You think I'm being ridiculously romantic, don't you?' she said with a tired smile. 'Well, maybe I am, but I think I'm right. I didn't sleep at all last night,' she confessed. 'I just sat here, thinking about Stephen, and I don't think it would be fair on either of us to marry unless I'm sure that he's absolutely the right man for me. As soon as I admitted to myself that I didn't really want to marry Stephen I felt relieved, and I knew I was making the right decision.'

Searching for a tissue, she blew her nose defiantly. 'I don't know why I'm crying, really,' she admitted, shame-faced. 'I suppose it's the thought of being in my thirties and having to start all over again. Everyone seems to be married except me. What if I never find the right man for me?'

'You will,' Gray told her firmly, putting his arm around her and giving her a hug. 'It doesn't matter how old you are, you'll always be gorgeous and you deserve the best. It'll be your turn soon, I promise you. There's someone out there just waiting for you, and when you meet him you'll know that you were right to hold out for the right one.

'Don't settle for second best, Lizzy,' he said seriously. 'You'll never be happy if you do that.'

'I know.' Lizzy gave a rather watery smile and hugged him back. 'Thanks, Gray. You've always been such a good friend to me. I didn't mean to spend the morning crying on your shoulder!'

'It's here whenever you need it,' he said with another comforting squeeze. He didn't look at Clare. 'Come on, Lizzy, dry your eyes. You can have a shower and we'll make you a cup a coffee. You'll feel better then.'

CHAPTER NINE

IT WAS all very well for Gray to worry about how Lizzy felt, but what about *her*? thought Clare bitterly. Picking up the bowl from the highchair and scraping together the last of the cereal, she finished giving Alice her breakfast, her hands moving automatically but her mind elsewhere.

There was a hard stone lodged in her throat, but she refused to cry. She was *not* going to make a scene. If she gave in to tears and jealousy the way she wanted to, she would make herself look a fool and she would embarrass and alienate Gray. In spite of everything, Clare couldn't bear to do that, not after last night.

It was her own fault. She had let herself believe that their lovemaking would come to mean as much to Gray as it did to her. It hadn't seemed so stupid to hope that it might when Lizzy had been safely engaged to Stephen, but now Lizzy was free and everything had changed. It seemed very stupid now.

'Don't settle for second best,' Gray had said. That was what he had done. 'You'll never be happy if you do that,' he had said.

Tears stung Clare's eyes, but she blinked them back furiously. *She* was second best as far as he was concerned. Perhaps it was better to face reality than to indulge in foolish dreams, but it hurt so much more...

Mindlessly spooning cereal into an unusually compliant Alice, Clare wished that she could rewind time. She could have stayed in bed this morning, instead of walking into

the kitchen and seeing Lizzy in Gray's arms. Their image was burnt onto her brain.

Well, she had a choice. She could act the aggrieved wife, and appal Gray with unreasonable demands that he should have nothing to do with one of his oldest and closest friends, or she could salvage what was left of her pride and pretend that she didn't care what he did or who he loved.

When Gray came back into the kitchen, Clare was wiping Alice's hands and face with a damp cloth. 'I'm sorry about that,' he said carefully, his eyes watchful as they rested on her set expression.

She flashed him a brief, meaningless smile that was somehow more daunting than a furious tantrum. 'There's no need to apologise.'

'I got up when I heard Alice, and we came down here so that she wouldn't wake you up. I was going to bring you breakfast in bed, but Lizzy was here sobbing her heart out and I couldn't just ignore her.'

'Of course not,' said Clare. 'You really don't need to explain.'

'You are my wife,' he reminded her. 'You're entitled to object if you find me with another woman.'

'But I'm not a real wife, am I, Gray?' Clare removed Alice's plastic bib and lifted her out of the highchair. Setting her down on the floor, she gave her a box of plastic blocks to unpack. 'If we'd been married under normal circumstances, I expect I would have objected,' she went on in a deliberately careless voice. 'But as it is, I don't think it's any of my business. I understand how you must have felt.'

'Really?' Gray's expression was sardonic. 'And how *did* I feel?'

Clare met his eyes bravely. 'I imagine that it was very

bad timing for Lizzy to break off her engagement the day after you got married.'

Gray stared at Clare for a frustrated moment, before turning on his heel and crossing to the sink, where he filled the kettle and snapped it on. When he turned back to her he had himself well under control, although a muscle pulsing in his jaw showed the effort he was making to keep his temper.

'For the record, Clare, that wasn't what I felt at all,' he said coldly. 'I just felt sorry for Lizzy. She was very distressed when I found her. It's not an easy thing to decide to break an engagement.'

'She should know,' said Clare with a squeeze of acid. 'She's had lots of practice!'

His mouth hardened. 'That's not fair,' he said angrily.

'Isn't it?' Clare rinsed the cloth under the tap and wrung it out with unnecessary vigour. 'It's not as unfair as you encouraging her to hold out for some impossibly perfect relationship! We should have told her the truth, Gray. She wouldn't have thought we had such a wonderful relationship then, would she? God knows where she got *that* idea from!'

'She's just picking up on the sexual tension between us,' said Gray coolly, reaching for the coffee. He glanced at Clare, who had stiffened at the sink. 'There's no point in trying to deny it,' he said. 'Not after last night.'

Clare flushed and lifted her chin. 'I wasn't going to,' she said loftily. 'But being compatible in bed doesn't make the rest of a relationship perfect.'

'Believe me, Clare, you don't need to remind me of that!' There was an unexpected steeliness to Gray's voice. 'That spark of physical attraction is still an important part of any relationship, though, and no amount of friendship or

respect can replace it. If it isn't there between Lizzy and Stephen, she's right not to marry him.'

Of course he *would* think that, thought Clare miserably. He was only too eager for Lizzy to break her engagement, and it wasn't hard to guess the reason why.

She couldn't wait for the day which had started so happily to be over. As the morning wore on, an extraordinary number of people appeared, rubbing their faces, having found somewhere to sleep the night before. Glad of something to do to take her mind off the dull ache in her heart, Clare provided an enormous brunch for everybody, and afterwards she took Alice along to the airstrip, where they waved at the little planes as they took off one after another.

Lizzy was one of the last to go. She knew everybody at the wedding, and had no problem in hitching a ride as far as the airport at Mathison, where she could get a flight back to Perth.

'I'm so sorry about earlier,' she said as she hugged Clare goodbye. 'I really didn't want to spoil your morning.'

'It doesn't matter,' said Clare through stiff lips.

'You were both wonderful,' said Lizzy, moving on to hug Gray. 'You're so lucky to have each other. And as for *you*,' she said as she took Alice from Gray for a cuddle, 'you're just gorgeous!'

Delighted as ever by any attention, Alice smiled and bumped her head against Lizzy's chin. Lizzy kissed her wistfully. 'She's a lovely baby. Any time you want to have a proper honeymoon, I'd love to come up and look after her while you're away.'

Clare was taken aback. 'But…what about your job?'

'Gray was right about that cup of coffee making me feel better this morning,' Lizzy told her cheerfully. 'I've done a lot of thinking since then, and I think it's time I changed my life! I've enjoyed my job, but I've been doing it a long

time now, and I'm bored. I'm going to resign when I get back, and look around for something different, so I should have the time to come and help whenever you need me.'

Gray glanced at Clare's set face. 'That's very kind of you, Lizzy,' he said. 'We may well take you up on that. We can't go for a while yet…but maybe when Jack gets back?'

'We'll make a date,' promised Lizzy. 'And you two can have a wonderful honeymoon all to yourselves!'

Except that they wouldn't be going on honeymoon. She would be flying back to England, and Gray would have the perfect excuse to lure Lizzy back to Bushman's Creek to take her place. Clare's smile was brittle as she stood beside Gray, saying farewell to the last guests and agreeing politely as they told her how happy she must be to be married to such a fine man.

It was an enormous relief when the last plane buzzed along the airstrip and lifted into the sky and she could stop smiling. Clare was left standing alone in the red dust with Gray and Alice, while they watched the little plane until it was no more than a speck in the distance and silence settled slowly once more over Bushman's Creek.

After all the excitement, Alice was tired and fretful for the rest of the day. Clare knew how she felt. She just wished that she could scream and cry and throw things the way a baby could. By the time she got Alice into bed that night, she was exhausted.

'I think I'll go to bed,' she said, when Gray offered her a cup of coffee after a silent supper. The stockmen had Sundays off, and had all gone to the pub in Mathison, so she and Gray were alone. They had both made an effort to carry on as normal, but the conversation was stilted and kept petering out into an awkward silence.

'I'm tired,' she told him, and there was something bleak about the way he nodded.

'We're all tired.'

At least it was an excuse to lie in bed without touching. Clare thought about moving back to her old room, but that would only show Gray how hurt she was, and she was determined not to do that. Pride might not be much of a comfort, but it was all that she had.

So she lay with her back to Gray, and pretended to be asleep when he came to bed in his turn.

She could hear him moving quietly around the dark room. She willed herself to sleep, but how could she relax when the darkness vibrated with the sound of him undressing? She could picture him so clearly, tugging his shirt out of his trousers, unbuckling his belt, pulling off his boots, and she squeezed her eyes shut in a vain attempt to push the tantalising image away.

The bed dipped as he got in beside her, and Clare tensed, longing for him to reach for her, dreading it at the same time, terrified that she would give herself away completely the moment he touched her. She sensed him glance at her and hesitate, but no deep voice murmured her name to see if she were awake, no warm hand slid tantalisingly over the curve of her hip, no kisses were pressed along her shoulder until she melted and turned into his arms.

Clare stared desolately at the dark wall, achingly aware of Gray only inches away from her. All she had to do was roll over, and she could press herself against the hard security of his body. She could run her hands over his warm, sleek skin and feel the steely power of the muscles beneath. She could slide her arms around him and kiss him and tell him that she didn't mind being second best.

But she did mind. Clare imagined Gray lying still and remote beside her, his hands behind his head, remembering

Lizzy and the fact that now she was free, and she knew that she couldn't do it.

Her body buzzed with exhaustion, but she was too tired and miserable to relax, and she had only just dropped into a restless sleep when the sound of Alice crying woke her instantly and she stumbled out of bed. In the end, none of them got much sleep. Hardly had Clare or Gray groped their way back to bed than Alice would start screaming again, and by morning they were all shattered.

The next few days were no better. Clare worried that Alice might be ill, and Gray dropped everything to fly them in to see the doctor in Mathison, but they flew back to Bushman's Creek none the wiser. 'It's just a phase,' the doctor told Clare, which she supposed was meant to be reassuring, although the only reassurance she cared about by then was a good night's sleep.

She and Gray took it in turns to get up to Alice in the night, but Clare still felt like a zombie during the day. Her head felt tight, her mind fuzzy, her body clumsy and heavy. She dropped flour all over the floor, put sugar in the gravy instead of salt, and would find herself standing in the middle of the kitchen, an onion in her hand, and absolutely no idea of what she had planned to do with it.

In an odd way, though, Clare was grateful for those disturbed nights. The sheer exhaustion made it easier to be normal with Gray again. They were both too tired to talk, or even to think, and there was no constraint between them when they crashed into bed to snatch what sleep they could before Alice got them up to spend the night walking endlessly around her room.

Just when they had forgotten what it was like not to feel that terrible, dragging sense of exhaustion the doctor's advice proved to be right after all, and Alice settled back into her old sleeping pattern. Dazed, and grateful for the re-

prieve, Clare and Gray were too busy catching up on their sleep and starting to feel human again to waste any time talking about their relationship at first, and as they slipped gradually back into old habits, Clare decided that was all for the best.

There was no point in talking, anyway. Talking wouldn't change the way things were. And was being second best really so bad? She was in Gray's bed, if not in his heart. She was his wife. She could walk outside, shading her eyes against the sun, and watch him walking towards her with his rangy stride. She could sit next to him on the verandah and watch the moon rise, and see his slow smile gleaming in the darkness, and at night she could turn and know that he would be there.

It wasn't perfect, but then hadn't she told Lizzy that no relationship ever was? They were together, and Alice was sleeping at night. Clare told herself that she was content with that.

They had been married almost exactly a month when the letter arrived.

Gray had been in Mathison that morning, and Clare was sweeping the kitchen floor as she heard the ute draw up the bottom of the steps. She was used to the lurch her heart gave at Gray's approach, and by the time he appeared in the doorway with a big box of groceries that she had asked him to bring back she had been able to assume an expression of calm friendliness.

'Hi,' she said, trying to sound casual. She kept on sweeping so that it didn't look as if she had spent the whole morning listening for the sound of the plane overhead. 'Did you get everything?'

'Everything except fresh mushrooms. I bought tins instead.'

'That's fine.'

It was always like that now, Clare thought despairingly. Polite, friendly—not tense, exactly, but somehow guarded, as if neither of them was prepared to let their defences down completely.

Alice had been in charge of the dustpan and brush, making a very satisfactory noise as she banged them together, but as she registered that Gray had arrived she cast them aside with a crow of joy and crawled across the floor to his feet with astonishing speed. The determination on the little face as she beetled towards him made Gray and Clare laugh. If a mountain had been dropped in her path, she would have simply ploughed up it and down the other side to get to where she wanted to go.

Reaching Gray's boots, Alice clutched at the bottom of his trousers, and he scooped her up to throw her into the air. He was still smiling as he caught her, and his eyes went past her to Clare, who was watching them with an unguarded expression, the broom forgotten in her hands.

Across the kitchen, brown eyes met grey, and the smiles faded from their faces as the air evaporated between them, leaving a breathless, charged silence that set something trembling inside Clare. She couldn't have looked away if she had tried.

It was Alice, of course, who broke the moment. Disappointed at the end of her game, and sensing that Gray's attention was elsewhere, she batted his nose with her hand and closed the small fingers around his lower lip like a vice, so that he winced and jerked his head away. Delighted at the success of her strategy, Alice beamed at him.

Gray scowled with mock ferocity, but she only nuzzled into his shoulder, quite unintimidated, and by the time he had turned back Clare had resumed her sweeping, and her face was hidden by the fall of smooth, dark hair.

'I collected the mail while I was in town,' he said gruffly after a moment. 'There are some letters for you.'

'Oh, good.' Clutching at the diversion, Clare propped the brush against the units and went over to the box. A pile of post sat on the top and she picked it up, riffling through the letters with hands that were not quite steady. There was one from her bank, a couple from friends, and—

Clare froze as she recognised the bold black scrawl on the envelope.

Gray must have been watching her face more closely than she'd realised. 'What is it?' he asked.

'It's from Mark,' she said in an odd voice.

She stared down at the envelope. There had been a time when the mere sight of Mark's writing had set her heart pounding, when she would have given anything to have heard from him. Now, his letter only left her wondering how he had found her address.

Numbly pulling out a chair, Clare sat down at the kitchen table and turned the envelope over in her hands. This was from *Mark*, the man she had loved and who had loved her. Surely she ought to feel more than this?

'Aren't you going to open it?' The harshness in Gray's voice made her start, and she nodded without answering. Sliding her thumb under the flap, she took a deep breath and tore the envelope so that she could pull out the letter inside and unfold it.

There was silence in the kitchen as the silver-grey eyes moved down the page and onto the next sheet. When she had finished reading it, Clare laid the letter on the table and looked at Gray with a strangely unfocused gaze. Her expression was quite blank.

'Well?' he said roughly. 'What does he want?'

His evident hostility made Clare blink, and she seemed to recollect herself. 'He wants me to go home,' she said.

'Go home? Why?'

'Because he loves me.'

'He's supposed to love his wife,' said Gray, and the stinging contempt in his tone made Clare tighten her lips and lift her chin.

'You don't love yours!' she pointed out coldly.

They stared acrimoniously at each other before Gray's eyes slid away. He put Alice down on the floor, where she crawled back to the dustpan and brush she had abandoned earlier. 'It's different for us,' he said.

'It's different for Mark, too, now.' The silver eyes were bright with hurt. What had she expected? Clare lashed herself. That Gray would deny it and miraculously discover that he *did* love her after all?

'What do you mean?'

'Mark's getting divorced,' she told him in a cold, clear voice. 'He says that he and his wife have tried, but they've both agreed that their marriage isn't going to work.'

'And the children?'

'He doesn't say,' Clare admitted, 'but they both love their children. They'll try to make the separation as easy for them as they can.'

'I see.' Gray picked up the pile of his own letters and made a show of looking through them. 'So now that everything's arranged to suit him, Mark expects you to drop everything and run back to him?'

'No.' She smoothed out the letter on the tabletop. 'Mark's not like that. He just wanted to tell me that he loves me and that he hasn't been able to forget me.' Her voice trembled suddenly. Why hadn't Mark written months ago, when she would have wanted to hear it from him, and not from the cold, distant figure with the angry brown eyes who could make her heart clench with longing just by standing there looking through his post?

Clare drew a steadying breath. 'He wants to marry me,' she finished.

Gray's hands stilled at that. 'So...it's just what you've always wanted.'

She winced at the indifference in his voice. 'Yes, I suppose it is,' she said bleakly.

Gray gave up the pretence of looking at his letters and let them drop to the table with a slap that reverberated through the tense silence. 'Are you going to marry him?' he asked abruptly.

'I can't,' said Clare, turning her face away. 'I'm married to you.'

'I promised I'd end the marriage whenever you wanted.' It sounded as if the words were being forced out of Gray. 'If that's now, you just have to say.'

If he wanted to end it, why didn't *he* say? thought Clare wildly. She wanted to stand up and shout at him, to tell him he was blind and that she didn't want to go, that she wanted their marriage to last for ever.

'There's still Alice to consider,' she said dully instead.

'Alice is settled,' said Gray. 'You know that she'll be happy here.' He hesitated. 'If you want to go, Lizzy would come up and look after her. She's free now. She said on the phone last week that she'd resigned from her job, and that she could come up whenever we wanted. She still thinks we would be going on honeymoon, but we could tell her the truth. Lizzy wouldn't tell anyone.'

Obviously he couldn't wait to get rid of her. Clare felt sick, and there was a dull pain in her chest. Her hands shook as she refolded Mark's letter and slipped it back into its envelope with unwonted care.

'Thank you for the offer,' she said stiffly, 'but Alice is my primary concern. I'm afraid I'm not leaving until I've

seen Jack for myself. That's what I promised Pippa, and that's what I'm going to do.'

Unable to bear the disappointment she was sure would be in his expression, Clare couldn't look at him, but she could feel his gaze resting on her profile, and she averted her face to watch Alice, happily banging away with the dustpan and brush in the corner. Those brown eyes were too penetrating for comfort. She didn't want him to see the desolation in her face or the muscles in her throat working with the effort of not weeping.

'What are you going to tell Mark?' he asked heavily.

Clare looked down at her hands. If she had any pride, she would tell Gray that only Alice was keeping her from rushing back to Mark's arms, but the lie stuck in her throat. 'I don't know,' she said at last. 'I'll have to think about it.'

What if she was wrong about what she felt for Gray? she tried to convince herself when he had gone. What if this desperate, aching need for him wasn't real after all? She had found herself alone in the outback with an attractive man and a baby. Any woman might have fallen in love with him under the circumstances.

When she went home, as she would have to when Jack came back, she might find that her love for him was not what she'd thought it was. Maybe she would find that Mark was the man she wanted after all. Away from the outback, she would rediscover the noise and colour and excitement of the city, and she would forget Gray. Maybe one day this would be like a dream, and she would laugh at herself for having believed that she could fall so hopelessly in love with a man with whom she had absolutely nothing in common, a man who lived on the other side of the world in a place she didn't belong.

Maybe.

Clare got stiffly up from the table and began setting out

lunch. The men would be in soon, and the day still had to be got through, even when it felt if as the bottom had fallen out of her world. She had thought that she and Gray were coming to a new understanding, but it seemed that she had been wrong. He could hardly have made it clearer that he was tired of their marriage and wanted her to go home to Mark.

'I don't want to go home,' said Clare desperately to the cutlery in her hand, admitting the truth to herself. It was all very well to tell herself that she would learn to love London again, but it wouldn't be the same. It would be cold and grey and empty without Gray. How would she be able to bear it without him?

Don't think about the future, she told herself. Think about being here, now. There's still time. Anything could happen. Jack might stay away another six months. Lizzy might change her mind about Stephen. She might convince herself that she wanted to go home after all.

After lunch, Gray sent the stockmen out to repair fences while he retired to his office to deal with the paperwork that had arrived in the post. Clare put Alice down for her nap and went to sit on the verandah with a book. Normally she used the time Alice was sleeping to do the jobs that required a little more concentration than she could manage with a baby crawling around her feet, but today she was too tired to concentrate on anything. The chores could wait.

The book lay open and unread on her lap as Clare sat and gazed out at the creek, letting the stillness and the light soothe her jagged nerves. Slowly, she relaxed. It would be all right, she told herself. As long as she could stay at Bushman's Creek, everything would be all right.

In the homestead, she heard the phone ring, but she made no move to go and answer it. Gray was there, and she could sit here and enjoy the quiet.

When Gray pushed open the screen door a few minutes later, Clare was still sitting in the big chair where they had kissed so often in the past. She turned her head at the sound of the door, and her eyes were very clear and grey.

Gray stopped halfway down the verandah, just looking at her, and something in his expression made her get to her feet, a chill sense of premonition trickling down her spine as the book fell unheeded to the floor. 'What is it?' she whispered.

'That was Jack,' he said.

Jack. Clare stared at him. No! she wanted to cry. It can't be Jack. Not yet.

'Where is he?' she croaked, moistening her lips.

'He was ringing from Mathison,' Gray told her. 'He wants me to go and pick him up right now.' He looked bleakly into Clare's white face. 'He's coming home.'

Clare knew that she should say something. She and Gray had been waiting for this moment for the last three months. Jack was the reason she had set out from London in the first place. She had come all this way and now at last she was going to be able to carry out her promise to Pippa. But the only thought that circled frantically around her brain was that she wasn't ready.

She wasn't ready to find the right words to tell him about Pippa. She wasn't ready to give Alice to her father. She wasn't ready to leave Gray.

She wasn't ready to go.

'Will…will you tell him about Alice?' she said, finding her voice with an effort.

'He knows,' said Gray gently. 'He told me that he hadn't been able to settle after Pippa left. He did everything he could to forget her, even heading off to South America. He'd always wanted to go there, and he thought there would be nothing of Pippa there to remind him of her, but

he said it wasn't any good. He stuck it as long as he could, and then he gave up. He decided he had to go to England and see her.'

Gray paused, watching in concern as Clare sat heavily down in a chair, staring blindly ahead of her. 'Jack had your address from when Pippa used to write to you, and he planned to tell you everything and ask you if you would let him know where she was. But by the time he got there, of course, you'd gone. Apparently he spoke to a neighbour of yours, and she told him about Pippa, and the baby, and that you'd taken Alice to Australia to find her father.'

'That would have been Mrs Shaw,' said Clare numbly. 'She lives in the flat downstairs. She was very kind when Pippa was ill.'

'She was kind to Jack, too,' said Gray. 'When he heard that you'd gone to Bushman's Creek, he got on the first plane he could, and now he's in Mathison, waiting to come home.'

Clare drew an uneven breath. 'You'd better go and pick him up,' she managed. 'If you take the plane, you could be back in a couple of hours.'

'Yes.' Still Gray hesitated. 'Will you be all right?'

'Of course.' She bent to pick up the book and from somewhere forced a bright smile. 'I wasn't expecting him to come back so soon, that's all. I don't know why it came as a shock. I mean, this is the moment we've been waiting for, isn't it?'

'Yes,' he said again. 'I suppose it is.'

Alice was awake. A beaming smile lit her face as Clare came into the room, and Clare's heart cracked as she picked her out of the cot and cuddled her. Overhead, she heard the plane as it banked over the homestead and headed towards

Mathison, towards Jack. When it came back, she would have to give Alice to her father.

Clare carried Alice into the bedroom she shared with Gray, and picked up Pippa's photograph. Her sister's face smiled up at her while Alice played with her hair and bumped her forehead gently against Clare, in the closest she could get to a kiss. Anguish twisted inside Clare as she looked down at her sister. How could she say goodbye to Alice now?

'I don't think I can do this, Pippa,' Clare whispered, but her sister just kept smiling back at her. *'Promise,'* her voice seemed to echo in the quiet room, and Clare remembered how she had looked as she'd lain in the hospital bed. *I promise,* she had said.

By the time Clare heard the plane buzzing overhead as it came in to land, Alice had been fed and bathed, and was warm and clean and sweet-smelling. Clare held her, kissing her dimpled hands and her head, where the soft down had just started to turn into fine blonde hair, and her heart was so twisted with pain she could hardly breathe.

Outside, the doors of the ute banged, and there was the sound of urgent footsteps on the verandah. Clare swallowed and tightened her hold on Alice. The next moment came the familiar creak of the screen door, but it was not Gray who stood in the doorway. It was Jack.

Clare recognised him at once from the photo Pippa had treasured, although the laughter had gone from his mobile face, and he looked tired and drawn. He stopped as he saw her standing there with the baby in her arms, but his eyes went straight past her to Alice's face. Alice looked unwinkingly back at him with exactly the same brown eyes.

Clare's throat was too tight to speak. Neither of them moved for a moment, and then Jack came slowly towards them. There was an agonising pause until, unbelievably,

Alice smiled at him, a wide, trusting smile that showed off the two tiny bottom teeth. It was almost as if she knew that he had come to claim her at last.

The expression on Jack's face made Clare's heart contract. Until that moment she hadn't known whether she hoped or feared that Jack would not want his daughter, but it was impossible now to doubt how he felt.

'This is Alice,' she said, swallowing the hard lump in her throat and managing a wavering smile. 'Your daughter,' she added, and held Alice out to him. 'Take her,' she said.

Wonderingly, Jack took Alice, gazing into the small, trusting face before he looked back at Clare. For the first time, his eyes seemed to focus on her.

'Pippa...' he began, but his voice cracked and he couldn't go on.

Clare drew a painful breath. 'She wanted Alice to grow up with you,' she told him, and in spite of her efforts her voice wobbled. 'She loved you very much.'

Jack didn't answer. He just looked wordlessly at her for a long moment and then he lifted Alice against his shoulder and turned his face into hers, giving and seeking comfort as if the two of them were quite alone in the world.

Alice smiled at him, a wide, trusting smile that showed off the few new teeth she...... it was almost as though she knew he was her father..... in the face at least.

Her expression froze, Jack's face froze. Clare's heart contracted, then began to break.....she *loves* him, Clare realised, she knew.......... that Jack was not what she thought, that...

CHAPTER TEN

CLARE'S vision blurred, and she went blindly past them and out of the kitchen. Stumbling down the steps, she ran towards the creek, the hot tears pouring down her cheeks. Dimly she heard Gray calling her name, but she blundered on until she reached the shade of the gums leaning over the waterhole, where she faltered, a hand over her shaking mouth and her shoulders heaving.

Gray caught up with her moments later. Ignoring her attempts to resist him, he put his arms around her and held her closely, and after a while Clare gave in and wept hopelessly against his shoulder.

'I can't bear it,' she sobbed. 'Alice is *my* baby now! I can't bear to go away and leave her!'

'Then don't go,' said Gray quietly.

'I have to! I promised Pippa. She wanted Alice to be with Jack, and I promised I'd leave her with him, but deep down I never thought I'd have to do it. I let myself think that Jack would never come back, or that if he did he wouldn't really want Alice, but I saw his face just now, he does...he does! And Alice just went to him,' Clare wept. 'She knew he was her father; I'm sure of it. They've got each other now. They don't need me.'

'Alice will always need you,' Gray told her, but she shook her head into his shoulder.

'She won't,' she mumbled tearfully. 'I'm not Alice's mother. She belongs with her father. I should be happy that Jack has come back as Pippa wanted, and that he loves Alice already...I *am* happy...but I can't stop crying...'

Gray let her cry for a while. He was holding her just as he held Alice sometimes when she was crying, his hand rubbing soothingly up and down her spine. 'Remember what you said when you first came here?' he said. 'You told me about your job and your flat and how much you loved living in London. You didn't really want to leave them, and now you can go back. That's where you belong…and now you've got Mark to go back to, too. You can have what you always wanted.'

Clare just shook her head and wept, and he tightened his hold. 'I know it will be hard leaving Alice,' he said, 'but you've got a life of your own, Clare. You've done everything you possibly could for her, and now it's your turn.

'You deserve to be happy,' he told her, stroking her hair, 'and you will be once you're home again. You don't need to worry about our marriage. I'll make sure the divorce goes through as quickly as possible, and then you'll be free to marry Mark.'

Clare knew he was trying to comfort her, but every word was making it harder for her to bear. She wanted him to beg her to stay, not make it easy for her to go.

Struggling to control her tears, she pulled away from him and wiped her face with her hands. 'Sorry,' she said raggedly. 'I'm just upset at the thought of saying goodbye to Alice.'

'I know you are, but we'll look after her, I promise you,' said Gray with a twisted smile. 'You'll both be happy.'

Alice would be happy, but not her. Clare's eyes were dark with anguish as she looked back at him, but in the end she just nodded desolately. If Gray didn't want her, as he obviously didn't, she might as well go home. She had a life to go back to, and perhaps once she was back in London she would remember why it had once seemed so

important, but she wouldn't be happy. She would never be happy without him.

Clare laid Alice in her cot and bent to kiss her goodnight. Jack had watched the bedtime ritual closely, and he stood now on the other side of the cot, looking down at his daughter with an expression so tender that fresh tears crowded Clare's eyes. How could she resent giving Alice up to a father who loved her so much?

With a last stroke of Alice's head, Clare straightened and smiled at Jack. 'I'll let you say goodnight to her,' she said, and went out, leaving him alone with his daughter.

There wasn't much to be done for supper. She had made a pudding that morning, the frozen joint had been in the oven since before Jack had rung and Gray had offered to do the vegetables. It felt very strange not to be in the kitchen at this time of the evening, organizing her pots and pans so that everything was ready at the same time, going through her own little rituals.

She would have to get used to it, thought Clare bleakly as she went to sit on the verandah where she had sat so often with Gray. There would be no great joints of beef to cook in London, no shy men trooping into the kitchen, no unhurried talk of rodeos and rain. And there would be no Gray, sitting at the end of the table, with his sure hands and his slow smile.

Clare pressed the heels of her hands against her eyes and forced back the tears. She couldn't keep crying like this.

Jack came out to join her a few minutes later. He sat next to her in the chair where Gray usually sat, and for a while they looked at the creek in silence. The sun was setting in a blaze of gold behind the trees and the horizon glowed as if a mighty fire had been lit over the curve of the earth.

'I missed the sunsets at Bushman's Creek,' said Jack quietly at last.

Clare didn't take her eyes off the sky. 'I'll miss them, too,' she said.

'Clare?'

She turned to look at him, and her heart turned over at the anguished look in his eyes.

'Tell me about Pippa,' he begged.

Sitting in the fading light, her face burnished by the last glow of the sun, Clare told him. Pippa, she knew, would have wanted Jack to think of her as he had known her, warm and vibrant and full of laughter, so she glossed over the last terrible weeks and told him instead how Pippa had loved him, how bitterly she had regretted leaving the way she had, and how she had longed to be able to come back to Bushman's Creek to be with him and their daughter.

By the time she had finished Clare was crying again. Jack took her hand and held it very tight. His fingers were warm and strong, like Gray's. 'Thank you for telling me, Clare, and thank you for keeping your promise and bringing Alice to me. She's all I've got left of Pippa, and I'll look after her just as Pippa would have wanted, I promise you.'

'I know you will,' said Clare through her tears.

Jack gave her hand another squeeze and let it go. 'What about *you*, Clare? What are you going to do now?'

'Oh, I've got my life to go back to,' she said, making a brave attempt to sound enthusiastic at the prospect.

'That's what Gray said,' Jack looked at her a little doubtfully. 'He told me about your marriage and everything that you've done—for Pippa, for Alice…and for us,' he added with a serious look. 'I wanted to ask you to stay at Bushman's Creek, but Gray says that you've done enough. He says that you want to go home.'

Jack finished on a questioning note, but Clare avoided

his eye. Her hands were clenched together in her lap. 'I think it would be better,' she said. Gray hadn't wasted any time in arranging for her departure, had he?

'I wouldn't ask you to stay for ever,' Jack was saying hesitantly, 'but won't you think about spending a little longer here, Clare? I'm not asking for me, but for Alice. She still needs you.'

Clare shook her head. 'No, it's *you* she needs now, Jack. You and Alice have to build a life together, and I'm not part of it. The sooner I go, the sooner she'll adjust.' Her voice wavered, then steadied. 'If I thought Alice really needed me, I would stay, of course I would, but I think it's time for all of us to move on, and it's better for me to go while she's young enough to forget me easily.'

Jack studied her with eyes that were so uncannily similar to Alice's and to Gray's. 'Are you sure?'

She nodded, swallowing the constriction in her throat. 'I just know that the longer I stay, the harder it will be to say goodbye to her.'

'I understand.' Jack laid his hand briefly over both of hers. 'When do you want to go?' he asked quietly.

'As soon as possible,' said Clare in a low voice, wondering if Jack could hear the sound of her heart breaking.

'There is a plane to Darwin tomorrow morning. You'll be able to get an international flight from there.' He paused, looking at Clare's rigid profile rather anxiously. 'Gray says that Lizzy would come up and help until we can find a housekeeper.'

There was a tight band around her chest, another circling her throat. 'Good idea,' said Clare with difficulty.

'It would mean telling Lizzy the truth about your marriage, though. Would you mind that?'

'No,' she said desolately. 'It doesn't matter now.'

*   *   *

Clare took off her rings and laid them on top of the chest of drawers, where Gray would find them. She looked around the room, as if trying to imprint it on her memory, and then she picked up her case, strangely light now without any of Alice's things, and walked along the corridor to the verandah, where Jack was waiting with Alice.

For the last time, Clare picked up Alice. There was so much she wanted to be able to say to her, but she was too small to understand, and all Clare could do was hold her close and hope that Alice would somehow know how much she was loved. Alice snuggled contentedly into Clare's shoulder, one little hand curling around her hair, and Clare closed her eyes against pain.

'I won't let her forget you,' said Jack quietly. 'I'll send photos. And you can come back and visit.'

It wouldn't be the same. Not trusting herself to speak, she kept her eyes squeezed shut.

She heard the ute drive up, and the achingly familiar sound of Gray's boots on the verandah steps. 'Clare?' He touched her arm and his voice was very gentle. 'If you want to catch the Darwin plane, we'll have to go.'

Clare nodded, dumb with despair. She kissed Alice one last time and gave her to Jack, and then she turned and walked blindly down the steps towards the ute without looking back.

As if realizing for the first time what was happening, Alice began to wail, and Clare covered her ears in desperation. Gray threw her case in the back of the ute, and got in beside her. After one glance at her face, he switched on the engine in a vain attempt to drown out the sound of Alice redoubling her heartbroken cries.

'Please, can we just go?' whispered Clare, and he put the truck into gear and drove quickly off.

The tears poured unchecked down Clare's cheeks as she

stared straight ahead, her hands still pressed to her ears as if she could still hear Alice sobbing for her. She mustn't look back, she told herself desperately, until she gave in and turned for a final glimpse of the homestead and the figures on the verandah.

But the homestead, and Jack, and Alice, had gone, swallowed by the red dust bellowing behind the wheels of the ute.

Sick at heart, Clare turned back to face the front. This would be the last time she passed the creek, the last time through the yards, the last time along the bumpy track through the scrub. I must remember everything, she told herself desperately. Memories would be all she had left.

To her relief, Gray didn't try to talk. At the airstrip, he put her case in the plane and helped her climb up, and the touch of his hand was harder to bear than anything else. He had left the ute standing in the shade. It will be there when he comes back, thought Clare, but I won't be.

Even now she found it hard to accept. She knew that she was doing the right thing in leaving now, but a part of her refused to believe that she would never again bowl along the track in the battered ute. Never again would she walk up the verandah steps and let the screen door clatter behind her. She wouldn't see Alice learn to pull herself to her feet or take her first step or say her first word.

And Gray would be here without her, moving easily through the bush with his steady stride, narrowing his eyes at the horizon, brushing the dust off his hat, and she had left it too late to tell him that she loved him.

The Darwin plane was already waiting on the tarmac when they touched down at Mathison, its propellers turning in a desultory way. At least they would be spared the agony of a long farewell, thought Clare. Moving like an automaton, she bought a ticket from the man who appeared to

run the airport single-handed, for, having dealt with her ticket, he checked in her case and took all the luggage out to the plane, where he began to load it into the hold.

Gray and Clare were left facing each other by the barrier, the silence thumping between them. 'Will you go straight back?' she asked awkwardly at last.

'Lizzy's coming up from Perth,' said Gray, sounding strained. 'Her flight gets in a couple of hours from now, so I'll hang around and take her back with me.'

'Good.' Clare couldn't look at him any longer. She stared down at her boarding pass which she was twisting between her fingers. 'Alice will be fine,' she said, not sure if she was trying to convince Gray or herself.

'Of course she will.'

The hold doors had been secured, and the airport official came back towards the barrier. In his shorts and shirt and long socks, he had a typically Australian air of good-humoured competence, and when he opened the gate he began cracking jokes with the five other passengers as he tore the stubs off their boarding passes.

'Well...' Clare swallowed as they filed through and began walking across the tarmac to the plane. 'It looks like this is it.'

'Yes.'

They stared at each other dumbly. If Gray touched her, she would be lost, thought Clare, torn between longing and panic, but he didn't. She saw his hands clench, but he let her turn and hand her boarding pass to the man.

This was it, she realized in disbelief. It was really going to happen. He was letting her go. She felt numb, frozen, unable even to cry.

She stepped past the barrier and onto the tarmac.

'Clare?' Gray's voice had an edge of desperation, and as she turned a hot breeze blew her hair across her face.

Putting up a hand to push it behind her ears, she looked back at him, her eyes very silvery in the sunlight.

'Yes?'

'I—' Gray stopped in frustration. Behind her the propellers on the plane were spinning faster, and a stewardess was waiting impatiently for her at the top of the steps. 'Thank you, Clare,' was all he said in the end, sounding oddly defeated. 'Thank you for everything.'

Clare couldn't bring herself to say goodbye. She tried to smile instead, but it went awry, and she made herself turn and walk away across the tarmac before he could see the tears streaming down her face.

The door closed, the propellers began to blur, and the plane taxied slowly down to the end of the runway. It paused a moment, and then launched itself back down the tarmac, lifting into the air almost level with where Gray waited. Clare looked down as the familiar red earth dropped away beneath them. She could see the corrugated iron roof of the little terminal building flashing in the sun, the tiny figures behind the barrier craning their necks as they watched the plane bank and turn, but as it climbed higher and higher into the dazzling blue sky they receded into the distance until they were no more than specks, and then they were gone.

It was raining again. Clare looked at the leaden sky and the raindrops splattering against the window, and the memory of the heat and the light of the outback hurt her as it always did. She had been back in London a month, four long, desolate weeks. It should have been getting easier by now, but it wasn't. The longing to be at Bushman's Creek was a constant raw ache that sharpened sometimes to a pain so acute that it made her gasp.

She wanted to walk out to the quiet creek, and to sit on

the verandah and watch the stars appear in their millions. She wanted to be in the cool kitchen, and to hear Gray's boots on the wooden steps outside, to listen for the bang of the screen door before he appeared, brushing the dust off his hat and smiling the smile that clutched at her heart.

She kept a watch on the outback time still. At odd times of the day or night she would look at it and be able to picture exactly what he was doing. When she was lying rigid and sleepless in bed, Gray would be riding out, his hat tilted over his eyes, scanning the horizon thoughtfully. Or he might be checking a water point or putting a mob of cattle through the yards. Clare could imagine them all stopping for smoko, Joe rolling his cigarette, Ben greedily eating biscuits, Gray drinking his tea, quiet and contained as always.

And when she stood at the bus stop with her collar turned up against the damp, she thought of Gray lying in the bed they had shared, with the starlight seeping into the room. She knew how he slept, how his expression relaxed and his chest rose and fell in a slow, steady rhythm, and she ached for the sound of his breathing and the warmth of his skin.

She thought of Alice endlessly, too, and prayed that she was happy. She thought of the sharply outlined patches of shade in the creek and the eerie caw of the rooks. She thought about the heat shimmering in the air and the way light changed over the ranges. She thought about the sunlight and the stillness and the silence.

Nothing was the same now. The busy streets that she had once loved now seemed to close around her, making her claustrophobic. They were too narrow, too noisy, too crowded. Before, she had never noticed how constricted the horizon was in the city. At Bushman's Creek you were surrounded by space and light, but in London you had to look up to see a tiny patch of sky.

Clare sighed and turned back to her computer screen. She had to think of her time in the outback as a dream, and somehow put it behind her. *This* was her life. She had friends, a good job, somewhere to stay until the tenants moved out of her flat. There was no point in hankering after a dream, no matter how wonderful it had been.

It wasn't as if she hadn't tried. She had been welcomed back into the office with open arms, and she had thrown herself into her job in the hope that she would forget that she had once been content to wash and cook and clean and feed the chickens.

In the evenings, when she could no longer bury herself in her work, she made an effort to go out and do all the things she had thought she had missed at Bushman's Creek. She met friends for drinks, she went out to dinner, she saw the films and plays everyone was talking about, but nothing filled the yawning emptiness, and although she smiled and laughed and pretended to enjoy herself, inside she was numb with a bleak sense of misery and loneliness.

Mark had been Clare's last hope. She'd clung to the thought that once she saw him the old magic would rekindle, and she would find that her feelings for Gray were no more than an illusion, but it hadn't worked that way. He'd taken her out to dinner, to a restaurant a world away from the kitchen at Bushman's Creek, and they had talked, but like old friends, not lovers. Clare had looked at him over the table and marvelled that she could once have loved him so desperately. He was attractive, he was charming, he was everything she had once wanted, but he wasn't Gray.

Gray...the thought of him made her clench with longing. Abandoning the memo she had been trying to write for the last half-hour, Clare picked up the watch on her desk. It was almost half past three in London, but at Bushman's Creek the stars would be out. Gray would be asleep, his

chest rising slowly and steadily. Clare could imagine it so clearly that she could almost hear the sound of his breathing, and when she turned back to her memo the words on the screen swam blurrily before her eyes.

Blinking back the tears and clearing her throat, she picked up the phone as it rang. One long buzz meant that it was an internal call, and she didn't want to embarrass anyone in the office by weeping down the phone, but it was only Annette, the receptionist in the entrance area outside her office.

'Are you busy?' she asked. 'There's someone to see you.'

'Who is it?'

'His name's Gray Henderson. I asked if you were expecting him, and he said he didn't think so... Clare?' Annette paused, puzzled by the intensity of the silence at the other end of the line. 'Clare, are you there?'

Clare was staring at the receiver in her hand, unable to believe what she had heard. Very carefully, she replaced the receiver without answering and stood up, surprised to find that her legs would hold her. Moving as if in a dream, she went slowly over to the door, and opened it.

A man was standing in front of Annette's desk, a lean, brown man, who turned at the sound of her door and looked at her.

Gray.

Gray. Overwhelmed by a turbulent wash of joy and sheer disbelief, Clare hung onto the doorhandle for support. 'It *is* you,' she whispered.

'Yes, it's me.' His voice was just the same, quiet and steady, and she stared at him hungrily, as if he were a figment of her imagination and might simply disappear if she took her eyes off him.

He looked tired and unsmiling, and there was a strange

air of uncertainty about him that she had never seen before. Clare was gripped by a sudden terrifying conviction that he had come to break bad news. Why else would he be here?

'Alice…?' she asked, unable to put the thought into words.

'She's fine,' said Gary quickly.

Clare let out a breath, and the tension went out of her. Behind him, she could see Annette, looking intensely interested, and she swallowed and stood back to hold the door open.

'Come in.'

Gray hesitated, then walked past her into her office. She closed the door and there was a silence as they looked at each other.

'How are you?' asked Gray at last.

I'm miserable, I'm desperate, I'm lonely. 'I'm fine,' she said.

There was an agonizing pause. Clare moistened her lips. 'How…how did you find me?' she asked, even though part of her wondered in anguish how she could talk such trivialities when he was there at last and all she had to do was walk across the room to touch him.

'I asked Stephen. I remembered how you had talked to him about what you did, and I thought he might remember the name of your agency. He did.'

'Stephen?' Surprise helped Clare sound almost natural, and hope leapt swiftly into her heart. 'Are he and Lizzy back together again?'

'No, Lizzy is still at Bushman's Creek.'

Of course she was. Clare had been trying not to think about Lizzy. When she pictured the homestead Lizzy was never there, moving around *her* kitchen, sitting in *her* chair, smiling at Gray and seeing him smile slowly back.

Clare walked over to her desk and tidied some papers,

giving herself time to wipe the bitterness and disappointment from her face. Her head was bowed, the dark hair hiding her expression, but when she looked up at last her eyes were very clear and direct. 'What are you doing here, Gray?' she asked almost rudely.

Gray didn't answer immediately. He went over to the window and stood looking out at the rain, as if working out how best to explain, but in the end his reply was quite simple. He turned back to her, his brown gaze steady on her face. 'I came to see if you were happy,' he said.

Clare stared at him. 'Happy?' she echoed, as if she had forgotten the meaning of the word.

'Are you?'

What was the point of pretending? She shook her head slowly. 'No.'

'Why not?'

Clare hesitated. 'Why do you want to know?'

'Because I love you,' said Gray, so simply that she wondered if she had heard him right. 'I thought you knew.'

'No, I didn't know,' Clare's voice sounded as if it belonged to someone else. She stayed very still, afraid that she was dreaming and that a sudden move would wake her, back to the desolation of reality. 'Why didn't you tell me?' she asked unsteadily.

Gray lifted his shoulders in a hopeless gesture that wrung her heart. 'I didn't want to make things any more difficult for you than they already were. You made it very clear that you would never consider staying in the outback, and I could understand that. You're a city girl. Bushman's Creek has nothing to offer a girl like you.'

As if unable to face the luminous grey gaze any longer, he turned slightly to the window and put his hands in his pockets. 'I told myself that there was no point in falling in love with you, that it was obvious that you didn't belong

at Bushman's Creek, but the more I saw you there, the more right you seemed. I came close to telling you how I felt many times, but I was afraid that it would make you feel awkward, and then we went to Perth, and I realized what a fool I'd been to even dream about you staying.'

The quiet mouth twisted at the memory. 'You changed in Perth, Clare,' he said, allowing himself a glance at her as she stood, still rooted to the spot with wonder and disbelief. 'I so nearly told you how much I loved you that afternoon we made love, but you made such a point telling me that it didn't mean the same to you. And then you walked out of the bathroom and you'd turned into this glamorous, sophisticated woman...

'I didn't know how to treat you,' Gray admitted. 'You accused me of jealousy that night at Lizzy's, and you were right, I was, but I was jealous of you, not of her. I hated seeing you so comfortable with Stephen. I knew he would be reminding you of Mark and everything you'd missed at Bushman's Creek. You said how much you liked Stephen, and it was like a slap in my face. If he was the kind of man you found attractive, I knew you'd never want me.'

'But...' Clare found her voice at last '...but I thought you loved Lizzy!'

'I do love Lizzy, but as a friend, nothing more. I let you think that I did. At first because I thought it would make it easier for you to accept the idea of marriage if you thought that there was no chance of me falling in love with you, and later because I was stupid and jealous.' Gray walked across the room and took her hands, as if he couldn't keep away from her any longer. 'But I've never loved Lizzy the way I love you, Clare,' he said, his voice so deep it vibrated along her veins. 'The way I've loved you ever since I walked up the hotel steps in Mathison and saw you waiting for me with Alice in your arms.'

He looked down into Clare's face, and his clasp tightened at the expression in her eyes. 'I knew there wasn't any hope for me, but I hoped anyway. I told myself that if Jack stayed away long enough you would get used to the outback, and to me, but then that letter arrived from Mark, and all at once I remembered everything that he had to offer you and I didn't.'

'And then Jack came home,' said Clare slowly, and Gray nodded.

'Then Jack came home,' he agreed, 'and I had to take you to the airport and watch you get on the plane.'

Clare remembered the beating heat and the smell of fuel and the desolation in her heart as she had walked across the tarmac. 'I thought you wanted me to go,' she said, still hardly able to believe that this was real.

'I thought *you* wanted to go,' said Gray. 'You had everything you said you wanted to go back to. You'd given up so much, Clare, I thought you'd earned the chance to have what *you* wanted. That's why I didn't say anything at the airport. I knew how hard it had been for you to leave Alice, and I thought you'd jump at any excuse to go back to her right then.

'I didn't want Alice to be the reason you came back, Clare,' he told her quietly. 'I wanted you to come back to me. I wanted you to be happy.'

'Gray...' Something hard and tight had relaxed inside her, and Clare could feel the happiness spreading through her, seeping into the ice around her heart, dissolving the pain and misery with its warmth, prickling her eyes. 'Gray,' she asked gently, 'how could I be happy without you?'

His fingers tightened so convulsively that it hurt, but Clare didn't mind. She smiled up at him through her tears. 'I said I was fine, but I haven't been. I've been miserable. I've missed Bushman's Creek, but most of all I've missed

you. There hasn't been a minute since I left that I haven't wished I'd had the courage to tell you how much I loved you.'

'You love me?' Gray released her hands so that he could cup her face wonderingly. 'Clare, how can you love me?'

'I don't know,' she said, her smile wavering. 'I just know that I do.'

He kissed her then, and with a sigh of release Clare melted into him, giddy with the relief of knowing that he was there, and that he loved her. She put her arms around his waist, the flat of her hands moving feverishly over his back as if to convince herself that he was real, while they kissed hungrily, and Gray held her possessively against him.

'God, Clare, I've missed you so much!'

Gray's voice was so ragged and shaken as he kissed her throat, her eyes, her mouth that Clare hardly recognised it. She clung to him, kissing him back with a kind of desperation.

'Why didn't you come for me sooner?' she asked breathlessly between kisses. 'I've been so unhappy!'

'I know, I know…' Gray lifted his head to smooth her hair away from her face with both hands. 'Lizzy said that I should come and find you straight away. She couldn't believe it when she heard why you'd gone. She said it didn't matter why we'd got married, that we belonged together, and that I'd been a fool to let you go at all. And Jack said the same thing.'

He looked seriously down into Clare's eyes. 'Jack's never forgiven himself for having let Pippa go. He knows what it's like to love someone and lose them because of stupid pride.'

'So why didn't you come when they told you to?'

'Because I didn't think they were right when they told

me that you loved me. You'd been so insistent that you'd only ever thought of our marriage as temporary, and although there were times when I was sure that you were happy at Bushman's Creek, you kept telling me you were a city girl at heart.'

He wiped the traces of tear marks from her cheeks very tenderly with his thumbs. 'I could have persuaded you to stay, but what would have happened if you'd started to miss your life here after a while? I didn't want you to wonder if you would have been happy married to Mark, or to feel frustrated because you were stuck in the outback when you could have been doing a job you loved.

'You had to have a chance to find out what you really wanted, Clare. After everything you'd done, you needed some time to think about yourself. I told Jack and Lizzy that you needed a month at least, and then I'd come for myself and see for myself whether you were happy or not.

'I nearly lost my nerve when I saw you,' he confessed, gesturing at her neat suit. 'You looked so stylish and professional dressed like that. I was glad I'd brought the divorce papers with me as an excuse to see you. They needed our signatures, and if you'd seemed happy I would have left it at that. I'd have known that there was no point in asking if you loved me as much as I love you.'

Clare smiled, 'And now that you know that I do?' she asked softly.

'We can tear the papers up.' Gray reached in his pocket and produced the rings she had left on the chest on the terrible day when she had thought that she would never see Bushman's Creek again. 'Look what I brought with me.'

'My rings!' Clare sighed with happiness as he slid them back where they belonged on her finger. 'I've missed them,' she told him.

'You'll always be able to wear them now,' Gray prom-

ised her. He smiled down at her, the smile she had dreamed about. 'Now you know why I wanted to buy you a diamond ring, Clare. I bought it because I love you, because I always will.'

Clare's eyes were luminous with happiness as she slid her arms around his neck and lifted her face for his kiss. 'Gray?' she said when she could speak, leaning back to look up at him. 'Will you do something for me?' she asked.

'Anything,' said Gray, holding her as if he would never let her go.

'Will you take me home?'

'Where is home?' he asked, and her smile was misty with longing.

'Bushman's Creek.'

On her first evening back at Bushman's Creek, Clare and Gray walked hand in hand along the creek in fading light. The sky was afire and the setting sun burnished the landscape with an eerie glow while the squabbling birds overhead fell gradually silent. Jack was putting Alice to bed, and Lizzy was in the kitchen.

'It feels funny not having anything to do,' said Clare.

Gray's eyes glinted down at her. 'Lizzy's going back to Perth in a couple of days. You'll have plenty to do then.'

'Now I see why you wanted me back!' she teased. 'You need a new housekeeper.'

Gray stopped and pulled her round to face him. 'I don't need a housekeeper,' he said, suddenly serious. 'I need *you*. I need to see you and to touch you and to know that when I come home at the end of the day you'll be there.'

'I'll always be there,' promised Clare, and they kissed as the sun slid slowly below the horizon.

'You know Jack's thinking of buying a property of his

own nearby?' said Gray, when they turned back towards the homestead. 'He won't want to be separated from Alice, so when he goes he'll take her with him. Will you mind losing her again?'

Clare thought about it, but not for long. 'A bit, but it won't be as bad this time. I won't have to say goodbye the way I had to before. I'll still see her if they're nearby, and they adore each other so much that it's much better for them to be together. And as long as I'm with you I don't mind anything,' she told him.

In the distance, the lights of the homestead shone welcomingly in the gathering darkness. Her footsteps slowed and she stopped, thinking about Alice. 'It will be funny without a baby to look after, though,' she added a little wistfully.

Gray's smile gleamed in the dusk as he drew her towards him. 'I expect we can do something about that,' he said.

What happens when you suddenly
discover your happy twosome is about
to turn into a...*family?*
Do you laugh?
Do you cry?
Or...do you get married?

The answer is all of the above—and plenty more!

Share the laughter and tears with
Harlequin Romance® as these
unsuspecting couples have to be

When parenthood takes you by surprise!

Authors to look out for include:

Caroline Anderson—DELIVERED: ONE FAMILY
Barbara McMahon—TEMPORARY FATHER
Grace Green—TWINS INCLUDED!
Liz Fielding—THE BACHELOR'S BABY

Available wherever Harlequin books are sold.